Praise for Kr

"Kristopher Triana writes beautiful nightmares, horrific fairytales, and intoxicating horrors, and however depraved and damaged his characters, you get to know them well… whether you want to or not." - Tim Lebbon, author of *The Last Storm*

"Triana's masterful, gripping storytelling will not let go… I'm blow away with what Triana can do and will read just about anything he puts out." - Scream Magazine

"Kristopher Triana's work is a volatile mixture of visceral noir and twistedly disturbing passion play that invades the reader's psyche and exposes the raw and throbbing nerve hidden within. His prose is unapologetic and totally without restraint or mercy. There's no denying it. Triana is the Master of Extreme Horror!" - Ronald Kelly, author of *Fear, The Saga of Dead-Eye,* and *Southern Fried & Horrified*

"Kristopher Triana is without question one of the very best of the new breed of horror writers." -Bryan Smith, author of *Depraved*

"Whatever style or mode Triana is writing in, the voice matches it unfailingly." - Cemetery Dance Magazine

"One of the most exciting and disturbing voices in extreme horror in quite some time. His stuff hurts so good." - Brian Keene, author of *The Rising*

"Kristopher Triana pens the most violent, depraved tales with the craft of a poet describing a sunset, only the sunset has been eviscerated, and dismembered, and it is screaming." - Wrath James White, author of *The Resurrectionist*

Recap of *Gone to See the River Man*

Lori only wanted to bond with convicted serial killer Edmund Cox. Taking her disabled sister Abby along, she journeys upriver with the help of Buzz, a hermit the sisters met while hiking through the woods in search of the mysterious figure known only as The River Man. Edmund has sent Lori to him to deliver a key, which she finds in Edmund's old shack, buried inside the chest of a rotting female corpse.

While searching for The River Man, Lori is confronted by her own personal demons. Once the river turns to blood, Buzz insists they turn back, and a struggle ensues. Abby hits Buzz over the head with her crutch, killing him. Lori and her sister then dump the old man into the river, where his body ends up crushed against jagged rocks.

Finally reaching the dark shack on the edge of the cliff, Lori meets The River Man, and he instructs her to finish what she started before she can go on to a new life with Edmund. In a jealous rage, Lori nearly killed her sister when they were teenagers. Now she finishes the job by pushing Abby off the cliff and down to the rocky waters below.

Lori returns home to find Edmund has escaped Varden Prison, and he is waiting for her in her apartment. He's killed another one of his groupies, Niko, and dismembered the body. When Lori approaches Edmund, he tells her it's time for her to reap the rewards of her quest, to get what she deserves.

"Will it hurt, darling?" she asks.

Edmund flicks the blade of his knife. "Love always does."

Along the River of Flesh

Kristopher Triana

Along the River of Flesh Copyright © 2023 Kristopher Triana.

ISBN: 978-1-961758-01-8

Cover Art by Lynne Hansen.

For signed books and merchandise visit:
TRIANAHORROR.COM

In loving memory of my father

"As long as people have problems, the blues can never die."

—B.B. King

PROLOGUE

LOVE IS A GHOST STORY, and the heart is its haunted house.

If there's life after death, I'll be callin' your name from Hell. I could sing to you. Play a lil' love song. You'd hear my voice echo through the pines, down in the valley low, with a guitar strummin' a special tune. But it'd really be the same ol' song—that sweet ol' music that comes down from his shack above the river and rolls on outta his world.

Hill country blues. Devil's music.

You'll hear me callin', just as I hear you callin' on me now. Your sweet nothings. Your baby coos. And your screams. So many screams, like a human slaughterhouse in my skull. It is the song from his world, sung in chorus—all my darlin' precious ones joined in a choir of blood.

And the blood runs like a river. And the river is our home.

ONE

"IT DOESN'T MATTER HOW LONG you've been on the job," Wright said, "when you fatally shoot someone, it has psychological repercussions."

Keith Drakeson slouched in the chair, elbows on his knees, his loose tie swaying. Last night's drinking made it difficult to keep his head up, but he kept his bloodshot eyes on his commanding officer. The lighting in Captain Shanice Wright's office was fluorescent, a sickly hospital color that, combined with a strange egg-like smell, made Keith queasy. His captain looked gray beneath these bulbs, like she'd aged ten years. Keith figured he looked far worse.

"C'mon now," he said. "Isn't it enough that I'm on administrative leave? I mean, a head shrinker? Really?"

The captain nodded. "Trust me on this, Keith. It's not just protocol, it's beneficial. Especially after all you had to see."

He knew the rules. After killing a suspect in the line of duty, an officer, even a detective like himself, had to be put on leave while the incident was investigated. Keith hated being off the job, but he could accept it. What he had trouble with was the idea of lying down on a couch to share his feelings with a stranger. There were too many things about himself he needed to keep clandestine.

"A lot of cops struggle with this sort of traumatic event," Wright said. "Working with a professional can help you."

"But I feel fine."

"Maybe you think so now, but the weight of this can haunt you for a long time. I've seen a lot of cops resign after something like this because they can't handle the emotional toll."

Keith scoffed. "That's not gonna happen."

"Easier said than done."

She crossed her hands upon her desk, over the manila folder—Keith Drakeson's file. He eyed it like a cat with a field mouse, unsure what lay inside and fearing the unknown. He'd had his share of complaints filed against him, but those were from his time as a uniformed officer working for a rinky-dink sheriff's office, long before he worked here under Captain Wright and long before he'd become a detective. Wright ran her fingers over her wedding band, centering the rock so it caught the light. She was always so organized. Her mahogany desk shined, clear of clutter. Just a penholder, a nameplate, a miniature American flag, and a photo of her husband and children, the perfect nuclear family. Wright barely looked like herself in the picture. It was the only instance Keith had ever seen her wearing something other than a pantsuit. She was also smiling, which seemed aberrant somehow, like this was an uncanny doppelgänger instead of his captain.

"I've written it up," she said, removing a slip of paper from the folder like a doctor with a prescription. "You're to see McHugh tomorrow for your first session."

"*First?*" he asked. That meant there were more coming. "But Captain, I—"

"It's not up for debate, detective. Consider it an order. Ten o'clock. Second floor."

Keith exhaled as he took the slip of paper. His hand was so pale next to hers, and not just because she was black. He needed some sun and a much better diet. Only thirty-four and yet he had skin like a retiree. For now, he blamed it on the wretched lighting. He had more important things to focus on than his health, be it physical or mental.

But Captain Wright would not understand that. Keith was wasting his time trying to reason with her. He would just have to talk with the shrink and hope no one else would hear about it, that his shame would go unnoticed. He stood. "Yes, ma'am. I'll be there."

***

Sundown came early now that it was late fall. That meant happy hour came earlier too. Keith's idea of happy hour wasn't in a crowded bar, but in his home. He poured a double bourbon and took the tumbler to the kitchen window where he liked to lean on the sill and look out upon the neighborhood. Two children were riding their bikes down the sidewalk. Keith's mind flashed upon a frightened little girl with wet eyes, and he hissed at the memory, shaking his head to force the image from his brain. He drank deep from his glass. He didn't need Dr. McHugh, only Dr. Johnnie Walker. Scotch did more for him than talking things out ever could. But while he often preferred being alone, he was considering having some company tonight. The captain's advice about clearing his head was solid. They just disagreed upon methods of healing.

He drew his phone from his pocket and called Ava.

"Hey, Keith," she said, her voice high yet soft. "You lonely?"

"Lonely as I'll ever be."

"Well, I could be free," she said. "But I'd have to leave by nine."

"I can handle that. The usual?"

"Mmhmm."

His frown deepened. He'd thought he'd been making progress with Ava, but she continued to keep him locked in this stage of their relationship. She told him she'd be there in twenty minutes. Keith lit a cigarette and cracked the window. A touch of the crisp air hit him, but he couldn't enjoy it for long. The shouts and laughter of the cycling children echoed up the street like birdcalls, causing something to sink deep within him. He wondered if he'd ever truly been young. He stepped into the living room and turned on the TV just to drown everything out. A news program was on, a reporter standing inside a ruined prison cell block with a microphone in her hand.

"This is the aftermath of the full-scale riot that took place in Varden Prison earlier this week," she said. "Several parts of the building have suffered extensive damage, leading this cell block to be shut down."

Keith stood in front of the set, watching with the cigarette between his teeth as the image of an overweight man appeared on the screen. The reporter spoke over it.

"Robert Woodrow, a guard at the prison who was put in a coma after being brutally attacked by inmates, passed away this morning at Brighton Hospital, bringing the death toll to twenty-three, including guards and other officials, as well as prisoners, and two county police officers who were first responders to the…"

Keith waited for what he knew the newscaster would bring up next. When she did, he sipped his scotch as if in toast as the mugshot filled the screen.

"The search continues for escaped inmate Edmund Cox," the reporter said, "with police now working with federal agents in what has become a nationwide manhunt. Cox, a convicted serial killer responsible for the murders of over twenty people, is the only prisoner yet to be apprehended after the prison break. The state has offered a hundred-thousand-dollar reward for any information leading to his arrest, but officials warn Cox is to be considered extremely dangerous."

Not for the first time, Keith stared at the photos of Edmund Cox as they appeared on the TV. Dark hair with hints of wolf gray, eyes black as onyx in the purple meat caves of their sockets, his macabre smile like a skeleton's rictus. His hulking form was menacing, his body hair thick and whirly as it tufted out of his collar and sleeves. There was always a thin layer of grease upon him, an evil secretion rising from his pores like venom. In some ways, the maniac's mugshot was even more frightening than the photos of the gruesome crime scenes he'd left behind.

During the investigation into what the press had dubbed The

Hill Country Killer, Keith and his fellow detectives had spent many hours going over those gristly images. One mutilated woman after another, defiled corpses found in puddles of their own gore, some stuffed into confined spaces that should have been too small for a human body, others splayed out in the open like grotesque art exhibits. Keith had not just seen these crime scenes in pictures. He'd seen most of them in person. If anything, the boss should have sent him to a psychiatrist for *that* instead of the Josh Negus shooting.

Being part of the unit that had captured Edmund Cox was Keith's greatest accomplishment. He'd even had his fifteen minutes of fame in the press, although the focus went to his superiors, with Keith not permitted to say much. That Cox had now escaped seemed to strip some of that glory away, leaving Keith even hungrier for adulation to massage his famished ego.

Administrative leave, he thought, frowning.

With Cox on the loose, the department needed Keith now more than ever. But instead of searching for the infamous killer, he was practically under house arrest, watching the events unfold on television instead of being immersed in the most exciting manhunt since the Boston bombers, one he felt belonged to him.

He finished his drink just before the doorbell rang.

Keith walked through the living room in his bare feet, the cool hardwood floors doing nothing to soothe the rising heat within him. As he undid the double deadbolts, he kept one hand on the shotgun mounted beside the window overlooking the front porch. He peered through the peephole to see the top of Ava's head, her face distorted by the fish-eyed glass.

"Hey," she said when he opened the door.

She stepped inside and kissed his cheek. Keith smelled her hair, taking in the aroma of femineity before kissing her just below the ear, tasting her softness. So clean. So angelic. So young. Putting down her bag, Ava slid out of her winter coat and Keith stepped behind her to help her out of it. She wore a gray turtleneck with a billowy collar and jeans so tight she seemed poured into them, with knee-high leather boots as black as her hair. Her makeup made her mysterious eyes all the darker.

Keith was still wearing his office clothes. Gray khaki slacks, a white shirt with the sleeves rolled up to his elbows, a loose tie about his neck. He'd shaved at six that morning, but stubble had returned. He hadn't even bothered to freshen up or spray a little cologne on for her. Though he was trim with rugged good looks, he knew he wasn't appetizing right now. But he didn't need to be. Not with Ava.

"So whatcha wanna do?" she asked.

He put his finger through one of her belt loops and pulled her into him.

"Subtle," she said, cocking an eyebrow. "Just take it easy this time."

Keith put his face into Ava's neck, and when she turned her head, she saw the news program on the television. The reporter was now detailing Edmund Cox's crimes.

Ava rolled her eyes. "Jeez. Don't you get enough of this stuff at work?"

She wiggled free of him, grabbed the remote, and started flipping channels. Keith stood behind her, waiting, aching, trying not to get angry.

"You can put on whatever you want," he said. "Doesn't matter."

Ava kept flipping, her hip cocked, her long hair like a curtain dividing them. She settled on a movie starring Jennifer Aniston, then walked backward and plopped down on the couch, her focus still on the screen. Keith hovered over her like a parent about to lecture a child. Ava patted the seat beside her.

"C'mon," she said, her smoky eyes falling upon him. "This is what you want, right?"

Keith cleared his throat, though he had nothing to say. He put out his cigarette, sat down beside Ava, and put his arm around her. She nestled into him, her head on his shoulder, her hand making slow circles over his belly, fingers toying with the buttons of his shirt. Her eyes stayed on the television. Keith closed his eyes, intensifying his other senses. His fingertips on the fabric of her sweater. The lingering smell of her shampoo.

The warm weight of her pressed against him.

She'd been right. This was exactly what he wanted. This was therapy worth the money.

TWO

GARY ROLLED ONTO HIS SIDE and glanced at the clock on the nightstand. It was now a quarter past ten in the morning. After waking up at eight, he'd gone to the bathroom to pee, then came right back to bed to stare at the ceiling. He knew he would not fall back to sleep. He didn't even want to. It wasn't exhaustion that made him reluctant to get out of bed, but an urge to avoid the everyday world.

Being self-employed, Gary Chatmon made his own hours. The downside to that luxury was he often had no reason to set an alarm or hurry out of bed when the sun came up. This allowed the old, gray mule of his depression to sit on his chest every morning, pinning him to the mattress. Despite his lingering pain over Lacy, he would never acknowledge it for what it was, but he was aware of this murkiness within him. It was a dour visitor bearing gifts of apathy and bitterness, more trash to be added to the landfill of his soul. Some days it kept him in bed until the afternoon, but today he had something to get up for.

Gary swung his legs over the edge of the bed and sat there, rolling his shoulders and cracking his vertebrae before rising from the mattress, a zombie coming out of the grave. He never turned the heat on when he slept, and the chill of the motel room sunk into him, attacking his joints. He grumbled as he stepped into his slacks. Not even fifty yet and his knees were already turning on him.

Putting on a flannel shirt, Gary drew back the curtains to see what kind of day awaited him. Pale sunlight made him squint. The maple tree out front was almost bare, a few yellow leaves clinging to the base, the others having blown into the gutters. There was morning frost upon the car windows, giving the illusion of a snow dusting. It did little to make this neighborhood any prettier.

He stared at the greasy spoon across the street—*Dottie's Good Eats.* A small diner with an actual tin roof.

Only in Killen, Gary thought.

The small town was a like sepia photograph of some forgotten time, a backwater berg for hill folk and drifters. It had a population under a thousand, the ranch houses and river shacks giving one another a wide berth. The motel was in the downtown district, a rustic avenue of crumbling concrete, broken glass, and boarded windows. There was a barbershop with elderly men out front playing checkers, and an old dog beneath the table watching passersby with cataract eyes. There was a post office no bigger than a broom closet, a second-run movie house, and a country store in a dirt lot with a phone booth out front. The building furthest from the others was a juke joint with a cracked sign above the door: "Junior's."

Last night, Gary had parked on the other side of the road, watching Junior's as the Saturday night crowd gathered for live music and barbeque. Black patrons outnumbered the whites, but it was an even balance of men to women. No kids allowed. Sipping from his flask, Gary had listened to the southern blues music as it rose out of the place like a hypnotic thunderstorm. He took a few photos from his car, then headed on to the motel for the evening. He'd have better luck on Sunday, when the crowd wasn't so thick and rowdy, and people could hear each other talk. Folks around here were already standoffish when it came to answering questions. Best to not confront them with any while they were dead drunk and trying to have a good time. This world offered few paths to even brief moments of happiness, and from what Gary had seen in the town of Killen, joy was rarer and more valuable than diamonds.

Maybe that caused you to run away from your hometown too, Jessica, Gary thought. *Is that what happened? Did you leave for some place where you might find joy, where a person could have a future? Hard to think it'd lead you here.*

Stepping out into the crisp morning, Gary pulled his coat on tight and stuffed his hands in his pockets as he crossed the street to Dottie's Good Eats, the binder tucked under his arm. The wind rattled the pines like maracas, the other trees having succumbed to November's rust. The sky was the color of tombstones, the air cold and damp. Once, he'd thought of this time of year as romantic. Perhaps that's what made it all the sadder to him now. Solitary men were often victims of their own sentimentality, and nothing set the despondency reeling like a wonderful memory.

As he entered the diner, the smell of bacon lured him, and he sat in a booth in the back, the furthest spot from other people. Looking at the menu, he realized he'd just have to accept that the selections didn't favor a man who'd already had his first heart attack. A pretty, heavyset waitress came to him with a pot of coffee in her hand and a pair of pencils crossed in her bun. Gary nodded, and she filled his mug.

"You're a new face," she said.

"You must be used to that, being this close to the motel."

The waitress shook her head. "I dunno how that place stays in business."

"Maybe it's just a lover's lane."

She snorted when she laughed. She looked him up and down, sizing him up, taking in his buzzed gray hair and square jaw.

"You look like a cop," she said. "You with them F.B.I guys?"

Gary leaned forward. "F.B.I guys?"

"Theys the only other new faces I done seen in these parts come lately. Two guys. Weren't here long. You ain't with 'em, huh?"

"No." He drew a card from his binder and handed it to her. "Gary Chatmon. Private Investigator."

She smiled, amused. Gary noticed her chipped tooth.

"Well, I'll be," she said. "Just like that old show, *Magnum P.I.* I ain't never met no private eye before. Didn't know ya'll were still a thing."

"We're around, here and there. Right now, I'm here in Killen. Looking for somebody."

Her smile faded a little.

"Don't worry," Gary told her. "I'm not looking to get anyone in trouble. I'm actually trying to help someone. See, I'm looking for—"

"A missin' girl." The waitress looked away. "Yeah, I reckon so."

Gary furrowed his brow. "What makes you say that?"

"Mister, we don't see a lot of new faces 'round here, but we used to, for a time. And when folks did come, they were always lookin' for their sister or daughter or girlfriend or somethin'."

Gary waited for more.

"After what all happened," the waitress said, "there was a lotta hoopla in this here town. Reckon we're all glad to see it done with. Least we was, 'fore *he* got in the news again."

"Edmund Cox," Gary said, the name falling from his mouth like ash.

The waitress exhaled. "We don't like to say his name 'round these parts, mister."

"His known crimes weren't committed here."

"Yeah, but this is where he were born. Killen ain't known for nothin' else. Proud home of the nation's most famous killer since Jeff Dahmer. Not exactly somethin' we want on our town sign, know what I mean?"

Seeing the woman's irritation rising, Gary pulled away from the subject of Cox, for now. He drew a photograph from the binder.

"Listen," he said, "I'm not trying to dig up that past. I'm just looking for a missing teenage girl. Her family hired me to search for her. Will you just take a look?"

"Oh, alright."

Her shoulders sagged, but the agitation left her face. He

handed the waitress the picture of a skinny Chinese girl of seventeen with long hair and soft eyes. Her lips were full, her teeth like a toothpaste ad.

"Jessica Hong," Gary said. "From Maryville."

"Musta been missin' a while. That madman's been in the slammer some time now. Least he was."

"You recognize her?"

The waitress shook her head. "Sorry. I don't think I ever seen *any* Asian folk in this here town. Reckon that's why *he* left. That crazy bastard had a type. All those poor girls. It's a sin what all he done to 'em." She handed back the photo. "Now you wanna order somethin'? I don't wanna be rude, but I gots other folks to wait on."

Gary slid the photo back into the binder. "I'll need a minute."

"Sure. Sit a spell." She was about to walk away but turned back, her voice low. "Just a word of advice, mister—be careful. Killen ain't a good place to go snoopin'. You might end up findin' somethin' you wished you hadn't."

Gary nodded.

He was counting on that.

THREE

UNDER THE BRUISED AND ASHEN SKY, the river appeared ink-black, making Edmund think of contracts, of deals. He smirked and scratched his back beneath the denim coat he'd stolen from the Goodwill. The jacket was cowboy cut and paired oddly with his prison slacks, but it wasn't like people would look at him. He was steering clear of others during daylight hours. There was only one man he wanted to see, one deal he wanted honored.

"Home sweet home," he said as he stared over the rushing water.

Black gorge walls flanked the river, the dead trees poking out of the cracks like expunged veins. The rich woodland of Killen hadn't changed since he'd been gone, but then again, it hadn't changed since he was a child growing up in this hollow, catching squirrels for supper and playing folk songs on the two-string board nailed to the side of the shack. Even then, his favorites were the murder ballads—"Stagolee" and "Knoxville Girl" and "Down in the Willow Garden". From the time he'd learned to walk he'd wandered these woods alone, listening to the roar of the river, the clicks of insects, the call of unseen crows and owls. He'd set traps for field mice and tortured them with his folding knife just to hear them scream. Death had been the sound he liked most along this river, until he started hearing the music coming down from the cliff, a solo guitar that sounded both in and out of tune.

Hill country blues. *Devil's music.*

It was this that drew him to his calling, even before his uncle introduced him to his treasured photos—snapshots of war crimes that launched Edmund's sexual awakening. His dear uncle was long gone, but Edmund continued the work, carrying on the art of the Cox family.

He drew the wad of paper from his pocket and peeled back the flaps to get to the core. Some of the blood was still wet, the severed finger of one of his darlings still seeping. His other groupie's front teeth were scattered around it, and the bits of her gums where he'd yanked the teeth from her mouth were turning black.

"Pretty things," he said to these keepsakes.

Retaining pieces of his darlings kept them close to Edmund. It was as if he captured their souls as well as their bodies. That one of his women had given herself to him willingly made it even more beautiful.

"I feel you with me now, darlin'," he said to Lori's remains. "You're deep inside. You're comin' home with me. You'll be with me always now."

He pushed aside the finger to retrieve the dislodged eye. The iris was just as black as the pupil, the whites streaked with red lightning. He brought it to his lips for a gentle kiss, then stared into its peaceful void, catching his shadowy outline in the reflection.

"You see me in all the ways they couldn't," he told her. "You know my truth."

He enveloped his fleshy treasures back into the paper and stuffed the bundle in his breast pocket so his darlings would be close to his heart.

He started down the slope.

Ahead of Edmund Cox, the river howled like a thousand tortured souls, welcoming him home.

FOUR

THEY WERE LOOKING IN THE WRONG PLACES.
Fucking feds, Keith thought.

There was no way Cox would stay anywhere near Varden Prison after breaking out. He'd always been a traveler, a deadly vagabond. It had made him more difficult to catch. If not for the shared ethnicity of his victims, Cox's crimes might not have been linked. His methods of murder were always ghastly, but always different. A strangulation followed by a stabbing; a shotgun blast followed by a beheading. Chopped bodies. Pulverized bones. Genital mutilation. His only M.O. was in his targets—Asian women. Most were young, but he'd killed an elderly grandmother and another woman just shy of her fifty-third birthday. His youngest victim was a twelve-year-old girl he'd sodomized and dismembered. Her legs and torso were recovered, but they had never found her arms and head. The family had only identified her by her initialed sneakers.

And now he was loose again. The blood would flow like a river.

River, Keith thought.

They'd found no victims in Cox's hometown of Killen. They'd also been unable to pin down any known address. Some believed there was a shack out there on the Hollow River, but most thought it was only urban legend, a haunted house story for the children of that sorry, backwoods community. But Edmund was a talker, and Keith and his partner had questioned him at length, hoping to find more bodies.

"There's no place like home," Edmund had told them as they sat across from him in the interrogation room. "That were one my favorite movies what when I was a kid. *The Wizard of Oz.* Dorothy followed that yellow brick road, meetin' many magic strangers along the way in search for the wizard."

"Is that how you see yourself?" Keith asked. "As a wizard?"

Edmund chuckled. "Nah. I ain't him. I'm Dorothy."

Keith looked to his partner, Darius Clay, sharing a puzzled glance. The detective was a wide-shouldered black man from Chicago, a real no-nonsense bull. He was showing great restraint by tolerating Edmund's seemingly pointless anecdotes.

"You followed a yellow brick road?" Keith asked.

"Followed the river," Edmund said with a twisted smile. "Ya'll got religion?"

The detectives only stared at the madman. Keith felt suddenly empty, like a helium balloon released from a child's hand. The sensation passed as quickly as it came but left a lingering unease.

"Where I come from," Edmund said, "we use to done play them spirituals." He clapped his hands and sang in a low voice. *"Gonna stick my sword in the golden sand—down by the riverside. Down by the riverside. Down by the riverside. Gonna climb up on that mountain—down by the riverside. Down by the riverside. Down by the riverside."* He stopped clapping. "Most folk think that song's about bein' baptized, but folks in Killen know the real truth."

"And what truth is that?" Darius asked.

Edmund fell silent before answering. "Well, it sure ain't Jesus."

Thinking back on this, Keith finished his fourth cup of black coffee and went to the anteroom to put on his shoes. He was still wearing the same clothes from yesterday, but at least he'd shaved and combed his hair. That was enough for Dr. McHugh.

It was another cold, gray morning, matching Keith's mood

as he drove his work route, his mind returning to thoughts of Edmund Cox. The man was *his* perp. To think of someone else bringing him in made Keith's teeth grind.

At a red light, he looked at himself in the rear-view mirror, staring into his own eyes. Instead of a window to the soul, he saw an emptiness that disturbed him, causing him to look away.

There was a sudden, loud noise.

A gunshot.

The sound came again, and Keith realized it was not a gun, but a horn honking. He looked up and saw the light was green. The person behind him was in a hurry. They must have had somewhere better to go than he did.

When Keith arrived at the shrink's office, he whispered his name to the receptionist, not wanting the other people in the waiting room to know who he was. He sat down and stared at the carpet, not bothering to check his phone or thumb through the magazines on the table. He sat like that for what felt like a very long time. When finally he was allowed entry, his grudge had swelled, and when they shook hands, he gripped Dr. McHugh's a little tighter than normal. The psychiatrist was a short, balding man with a thin, white beard and a paunch. He wore granny glasses and when he sat down and crossed his legs, Keith spotted tie-dye socks hiding beneath his otherwise professional attire.

"Well now," McHugh said. "Detective Drakeson. May I call you Keith?"

Keith nodded. Maybe if he played nice, he could cut some hours from these sessions and get back to work sooner.

"So," Keith said. "Guess you wanna hear about the shooting."

"If that's what you'd like to talk about."

"That's what I'm here for, isn't it?"

The doctor readied his notepad and pencil. "We don't have to jump right into the incident. We can talk about whatever you like. But if you want to start with the shooting, we certainly can. This is your time, Keith. I want you to feel comfortable."

Instead of lying back on the couch, Keith sat forward, his

elbows on his knees. The sooner he shared his supposed feelings about the death of Josh Negus, the sooner he'd be out of here.

"Negus was part of a human trafficking ring," he said. "Sex slavery."

He expected some sort of reaction from McHugh, but the man's beady eyes remained dull behind his glasses.

"I was tipped off by an informant to Negus' whereabouts and decided to check it out. So, I went to this apartment over eastside."

"Alone?" McHugh asked.

"Yeah. I had reason to believe Negus was on the move. I needed to get there quickly if I was gonna catch him."

You also make arrests for yourself, Keith thought. *You want that glory. You* deserve *it.*

"When I arrived," Keith said. "Negus was there. And he had a child inside."

McHugh was stoic, silent, watching Keith with a stale expression.

"The bastard panicked when I pounded on the door," Keith said. "I heard the kid screaming, so I kicked the door in and drew my pistol. Negus was standing there, holding a gun to the head of an eight-year-old girl." Keith swallowed hard. "When I told him to drop it, he told me to eat shit. I tried to get him to calm down and let the girl go. I couldn't shoot him because the girl was his human shield. I told him he didn't have to do this, that we could talk things out. He only laughed and called me a lying pig. The crazy bastard seemed wired on something, you know? High as a fuckin' kite. Excuse my language."

McHugh nodded. "It's fine."

"So, I tried to reason with the son of a bitch, but he was crazy, a maniac. There was nothing I could do… he… he shot the girl in the head. Right there in front of me."

He let that sit on McHugh's shoulders. The doctor seemed a little uneasy now, and it pleased Keith to see him discomforted. This twerp couldn't last a day in Keith's shoes, but he was supposed to talk cops through their problems? Pathetic.

"He dropped the girl's body toward me," Keith continued,

"trying to slow me down so he could take a shot at me. That's when I fired."

McHugh fidgeted with his pencil but scribbled nothing down. Keith had expected a bigger reaction from the shrink.

"That's pretty much it," Keith said. "I shot a child killer, and now I'm on forced leave."

"That angers you?" McHugh asked. "Being forced to take a leave?"

"Shit yeah. I've worked too long and hard to get where I am to have other people tell me I'm not fit to do my job. I made detective in my early thirties. That's no small achievement."

McHugh nodded. "How are you sleeping?"

The change of subject threw Keith off. "Alright, I guess."

"Worse than usual? The same?"

"Same, I guess."

"What's a normal night for you?"

Keith sucked in his bottom lip. He couldn't confess to his evening routine, couldn't tell the shrink a normal night meant heavy drinking and maybe a prostitute.

"I get between seven and nine hours sleep," Keith lied. "Unless duty calls."

McHugh jotted something down. "What about your dreams? What're they like?"

Keith never dropped his eyes when another man was looking at him, but he was tempted to now. Instead, he told another lie.

"I never remember my dreams," he said.

There was a brief silence.

"Tell me how you've been feeling since the shooting," McHugh said.

But Keith couldn't. "Like I said, I'm not happy about being on leave."

"I mean how are you feeling about the shooting itself."

Keith's mind flashed on the cries of a little girl and a bright burst of blood.

"I did what I had to do," he said.

He almost said he wished he'd shot sooner, that maybe he could have saved the girl's life if he had. But then McHugh would think he was depressed, that he felt guilty and blamed himself for what happened. That wouldn't look good on Keith's record and would only keep him on leave longer, so he kept his mouth shut.

"How's your home life?" McHugh asked, rerouting again.

"You asking if I'm married? Shouldn't that sort of thing be in my file?"

"I'd like you to elaborate."

Keith sighed—not a sad sigh, but an agitated one. "No wife, no kids, and that's the way I like it. No, I'm not gay or anything like that. I like the ladies. I just don't wanna settle down. It's too much like giving up."

McHugh's eyebrows raised, and he scribbled notes. It seemed this comment had interested him.

"I just mean…" Keith continued. "I'm just too focused on my career right now."

"Are you dating?"

Keith thought of Ava, the only steady woman in his life, one he had to pay for.

"Nothing serious," he said. "I have a few girls I see but wouldn't go so far as to call any of them my girlfriend."

"Do you ever feel lonely?"

Keith glowered. "Hey, what is this? Why am I being interrogated over my love life?"

"Does it upset you to talk about it?"

"I don't get upset, I get—" He stopped himself before he could say *pissed off*. "I get a little annoyed is all. I mean, I'm here to talk about work, not my personal life, right?"

"Both play a role in your mental and emotional state. After a traumatic experience, it can be very beneficial to have friends and family as a support group."

"And a shrink too, right?"

Keith told himself to stop making snide comments. Even though the little creep deserved to be put in his place, being standoffish with McHugh wouldn't help him get back on the job. Despite the doctor-patient confidentiality, Keith believed this man would give some sort of report back to Captain Wright, and Keith wanted it to say he was mentally sound, not angry and instigative. So, for the rest of their session, he gave the doctor what he thought would be the best answers, showing just enough sadness over the shooting to seem normal but not so much as to be deemed clinically depressed.

When the hour was up, Keith headed for the nearest bar.

It wasn't quite noon yet. The place was empty but for Keith, the bartender, and a waitress refilling the salt and pepper shakers. A fat, middle-aged man tended bar, breathing through his mouth. The waitress was college age, with long blonde hair and a toned backside in tight jeans. Keith watched her move about as he sipped his scotch, going down a mental checklist of all the things he'd like to do to her. There'd been a time he would have tried to strike up a conversation, but his days of pitching woo were well behind him. He was still a young man but found dating to be more trouble than it was worth. There were easier ways to get laid. He'd also been honest with the shrink about not wanting to get married. In most divorce cases, the woman initiated it, and then she got to keep the house, half the man's stuff, and even take his kids away. Meanwhile, wives weren't even wives anymore. They had their own careers and didn't keep house or make pleasing their man a priority. Keith couldn't understand why any man would even want a wife these days. It was simply a poor investment.

A TV mounted behind the bar flickered with a news program. Keith had no interest in politics or world events. It wasn't until a mugshot of Edmund Cox appeared on the screen that his attention left the waitress' ass. Though the sound was muted so they could hear Lynyrd Skynyrd on the jukebox, the program was closed captioned. Keith read along.

Cox has been the subject of a massive F.B.I search and is believed to be responsible for additional murders since his escape. Two women who were in constant communication with Cox during his incarceration—and officials referred to as "groupies" of the notorious killer—were discovered dead in an apartment complex, a crime scene the local sheriff called "one of extreme violence and unquestionable evil." The women—whose names are being withheld at this time—had been brutally murdered and dismembered.

Keith gritted his teeth.

"Lori," he whispered.

FIVE

THE HONGS SHOULD ONLY LOOK FOR CLOSURE.
Their daughter, Jessica, had been gone for almost a year. If she were still alive, she would be twenty-one now, but given everything Gary had gathered, that was a pretty big if.

Maryville—Jessica's hometown—wasn't too far from Killen. Only a three-hour drive. Maryville had a much higher population and was better developed, but that was true of just about anywhere compared to this backwoods river town. Gary hadn't told the family he was coming to Killen to continue his search. He was going on a morbid hunch, one based on the girl's ethnicity and her studies—and particularly, her essays. Jessica had been working towards a doctorate in southern American history and folklore. Before disappearing, she'd made several research-based road trips to rural towns. Usually she went with fellow students, but sometimes she went out on her own, always the overachiever.

Jessica still lived at home, but she'd vanished without saying anything to her family about going anywhere. While Jessica's car was gone, a search of her room revealed she had packed little, signifying she hadn't been planning to be away long. The Hongs didn't think their daughter would take a trip without telling them, but Gary believed Jessica hadn't expected to be gone overnight. He thought she was only supposed to be taking a day trip to a tiny town in the middle of nowhere. Jessica would snap photos of river shacks, dirt roads, and junkyard dogs, maybe interview a few locals, and be home in time for dinner.

But then she'd met Edmund Cox.

Of course, Gary had no evidence of that. It was just grim speculation. Just as he and the waitress had discussed earlier that morning, no known victims of Edmund Cox had been discovered in Killen, but this was the town he'd come from. The madman was born and raised here, somewhere along the Hollow River.

Considering all of this, Gary had researched Cox thoroughly. While nomadic, Cox hadn't gone across country in his rampage. He'd primarily stayed down south. In interviews done after his speedy conviction, the killer often brought up his hometown of Killen, but spoke in a strange form of redneck poetry, his comments nebulous and dreamlike, offering nothing concrete. Police and federal agents had combed through the woods of Killen in search of a potential Cox residence but hadn't been able to locate one. The Cox family had lived off the grid for generations, a private cabal of hillbillies who gave birth at home and lived off the land. They left behind few public records, and the people of Killen hesitated to say anything about them. Being the last of the bloodline, Edmund was the sole carrier of their buried secrets, and he wasn't prone to sharing them with reporters any more than law enforcement.

But Gary believed Edmund's attachment to Killen was too strong for the man to stay away for long. Southern men took their lineage seriously—just look at how they refused to retire the rebel flag. With all of Edmund's known kin dead and gone, the country boy would want to honor his roots. Even a murderer can be sentimental for the place they grew up. While Edmund wandered to commit his crimes—a smart tactic to delay being apprehended, as well as to find his preferred victim type—and though he often took residence in other locations, Gary believed the killer always returned home, eventually.

Before his arrest, Edmund may have been in Killen the day Jessica Hong arrived. Maybe they'd met at Junior's juke joint or Dottie's Good Eats and struck up a conversation, Jessica asking him questions about the town for research. Maybe he'd lured her to his home, some miserable shack along the river, promising to show her some antiques or southern artifacts. If the police couldn't find the place, what chance did they have of finding Jessica's body? She probably was buried in a shallow grave under the porch or locked away in a rusty tool shed. She might even be at the bottom of the river with rocks tied to her to keep her from rising to the top.

Jessica could be anywhere, but Gary felt certain she was somewhere in this town.

At least, whatever was left of her.

He didn't have the heart to suggest such a gruesome outcome to the family. Until he uncovered hard evidence, it would be better to let them believe their girl might be alive somewhere, especially seeing as Gary had only been on the case for a few weeks. After law enforcement gave up the search for their daughter, the Hong family had hired an investigator who'd milked them for months without turning up anything they didn't already know. Gary Chatmon was that asshole's replacement.

It certainly was an interesting case. Gary had done missing persons investigations before, but never one he suspected involved a serial killer. Most of the time he was investigating insurance fraud or staking out motels for photographic evidence of cheating spouses. This case excited him, at least as much as a depressed man was capable of.

His expenses included the cost of staying at the motel, and the room, while affordable, was a step up from sleeping on the cot in his one-room office, where he'd been living for almost a year without the landlord noticing. He had a hotplate and a mini-fridge, had a gym membership for the showers, and did his wash at the laundry mat. Gary couldn't stand to be in the house after everything that had happened, so he'd sold it just to have it out of his life. It got the bank off his back and allotted him a small nest egg for when business was slow. He always jumped at the chance to leave town for a while. Unlike those southern boys, Gary Chatmon wanted to forget.

Going through his notes on his laptop, Gary popped the prescription bottle and downed the anti-depressant with the soda he'd bought from the vending machine. He'd been on the pills long enough that they should make a difference, but the only noticeable changes were the common side effects. He'd gained weight and couldn't lose it no matter what he tried, and while he could still get an erection, he could rarely climax. Not that he had a sexual partner—he hadn't since losing Lacy—but people should at least be able to take care of their urges themselves. Instead, he often gave up while masturbating, which left him hesitant to even try. If the meds really had improved his mood, the extra layer of fat around his midsection and an inability to have an orgasm canceled out some of those positive vibes. Still, he kept taking the drugs, afraid of just how much worse things might get if he stopped.

Jessica Hong's personal documents were transferred to Gary's computer. She'd kept no journal, but there was a plethora of essays, reports, and other academic articles she'd produced. Gary was reading through them all despite the popular opinion that they contained no real clues to her whereabouts. As with most things, Gary thought differently than everyone else.

The essay he was reading now was titled: "Death Letter Blues."

It detailed the history of southern African American music, focusing heavily on Delta blues and hillside folk songs. The title of the essay was taken from the signature song by blues legend Son House, which was built upon his earlier recording of "My Black Mama, Part 2" in 1930. Many other blues musicians had covered "Death Letter Blues", including Skip James and a variation by Muddy Waters called "Burying Ground." This started the essay down an avenue of death-related blues songs and murder ballads of the twentieth century, as well as songs that referenced The Devil and black magic. Hong discussed the songs of Howlin' Wolf, Junior Kimbrough, Victoria Spivey, and Screamin' Jay Hawkins.

She told the story of Pat Hare, a Memphis bluesman who recorded a song called "I'm Gonna Murder My Baby", and then did exactly that, shooting down his girlfriend and a police officer in 1963. She wrote about Huddie William Ledbetter, who'd earned the nickname Leadbelly while in prison for attempted murder. One legend said he'd earned the name after surviving an attack where he'd been repeatedly shanked in the stomach. Then she told the legend of blues icon Robert Johnson going down to the crossroads to sell his soul to The Devil in exchange for guitar playing skills, and how Johnson, who'd been a relative novice, returned home an incredible guitar man, finding fame only to be murdered with poison shortly thereafter in 1938.

The grim and sordid history of hillside blues had surprised Gary when he'd first started reading Jessica's work. He'd only been familiar with more modern, mainstream blues musicians like B.B. King and Ray Charles. The genre had been stolen long ago by white copycats like Eric Clapton and Stevie Ray Vaughan, with *The Blues Brothers* movies turning it into camp. Gary hadn't understood the vast difference between Chicago blues and Delta blues. He'd been unaware of the Delta blues' dark roots, but it all made perfect sense when Jessica explained it. The people who'd created and performed that style of blues came from real poverty, pain, heartbreak, and horror. Mississippi had an appalling track record for its treatment of black people. The racist history was shocking even for a southern state.

Jessica had really done her research. The essays were incredibly detailed and informative, with credits to the works cited and web links to recordings of the songs mentioned. She'd made an online playlist, and Gary put it on as he continued to read through the Word documents, his study of Jessica Hong becoming a study of American history, music, and folklore.

He spent an hour reading before returning once again to the essay that had brought him to Killen in the first place, an essay that remained unfinished.

The title always made his skin pimple.

"Blood On the Water: The Twisted Legend of The River Man."

SIX

HAVING WORKED SO HARD TO get out of this godforsaken place, June had never thought she'd return to Killen. Being here was a harsh reminder of all she'd escaped—the poverty, the ignorance, the hopelessness only an awful town can produce. She'd wanted out of Killen even before her age had reached double digits, and she'd made several unsuccessful attempts to run away before succeeding at age fifteen, mooching and stealing what she needed along the way. Now June was eighteen—a grown woman by law—and had willingly returned to her putrid birthplace. It was amazing how times changed.

Killen hadn't changed though. It was the same squalid, broken-down, redneck berg it had always been and always would be, like an old, abandoned shithouse. As June walked along the cracked sidewalks of downtown, she gazed upon the southern slums with disgust. Crumbling concrete and rusted fences. Wood-rotted houses being swallowed by unforgiving wilderness.

June hated this place and everyone in it.

That Killen had spawned a prolific killer wasn't surprising. Living here instigated violent urges. How many fights had she been in as a schoolgirl? How many times had she fantasized about setting this fucking town on fire? So many daydreams of venting her frustration through bloodshed.

It was a cool November day. The breeze made her long, black hair flutter about her shoulders, and she drew the army coat tighter. She'd stolen it off a bar stool last spring, back when she'd been trying to make it in Charleston. It'd been just another dead-end town on a long list. June shifted her backpack. Her worn boots crunched the busted gravel beneath her as she crossed the street, dodging potholes on her way to The Sunshine Motel, surprised the place was still standing. The parking lot was littered with cigarette butts and glass shards from shattered beer bottles. One of the room's doors was gone, with black trash bags taped over the doorway with the words *KEEP OUT* spray-painted in runny, white letters. A possum scurried from behind the dumpster and darted into the surrounding woodland. June felt a certain kinship with this fellow vagabond scrounging its way through life.

The lobby was a small room with a counter and register. A portable, black-and-white television played a game show rerun. No computer, no chairs, no plants. The geriatric man behind the counter was skeleton thin but had a protruding gut that hung over his left side. It took June a few seconds to realize it was an untreated hernia. The old man's eyebrows were long and wispy, matching his beard, and he chewed on a wooden match as he welcomed her in. June lucked out. The Sunshine Motel was one of very few lodging places that didn't require a credit card, only a photo I.D. and cash advance. The old man couldn't afford to turn anyone away. She paid the forty dollars and was given a key—number three of only five rooms.

"Enjer yer stay," the old man said.

She felt his milky eyes on her back as she exited.

Though clean, the room was not much prettier than the motel's exterior. There were water stains on the ceiling and rips in the carpet. It was a non-smoking room but smelled like an ashtray. There was even a cigarette burn on the bedspread. The end table wobbled, and when she turned on the bedside lamp only one of the two bulbs worked. No Wi-Fi, only a clock radio and an old tube television with a hand dial. When she sat down, the bed groaned like a mechanical bull.

None of these flaws bothered June. This was just for one night. Tomorrow she would enter the woods—*his* woods. She'd only returned to Killen because that's where she expected him to go too.

Home sweet home.

"There's no place like home," she muttered.

June had read an article stating Edmund Cox was a *Wizard of Oz* fan. The magazine was in her backpack, along with the others. She'd read a lot about Edmund over the past year, trying to better understand the unknowable, but it was like attempting to solve a Rubik's Cube while blindfolded. Edmund was an enigma so foreign he barely seemed like a human being. Perhaps that's why so many referred to him as a monster, but June didn't think in such simplistic terms. She was aware of the nature of the man's crimes, but that didn't reveal the nature of the man himself. It was easy to call him evil but doing so failed to get to the heart of things.

The concept of evil was just a broad generalization people used to help them sleep better at night. It was easier to say someone was a villain than to try to understand why they would rape and slaughter innocent women.

Anything people couldn't understand they deemed crazy. June had learned that the hard way. She had few people in her life and had told none of them of her plans. Folks would have told her it was crazy to come back to Killen, especially with the goal she had in mind, but June was smart enough not to listen to others. She'd learned that the hard way too.

As she lay back on the bed, faint music came from the room next door. June kicked out of her boots and closed her eyes for a rest, letting the muffled melody guide her into a nap.

She'd always liked the blues.

SEVEN

PAUL CHECKED THE TINY BOX AGAIN, as if the ring might have disappeared. He just enjoyed looking at it. The gold band felt good against his fingertips, the diamond sparkling in the natural light. Hearing Shawna coming back from her pee break in the woods, Paul closed the velvet box and put it back into the front pouch of his backpack, where it would stay until the time was just right.

Shawna smiled at her boyfriend as she emerged from the shrubs. It was a look that could get Paul to do anything, and though he knew he was lost to her completely, he had no desire to be found. His love for Shawna had developed quickly and fiercely, and though they'd only been together for five months, he knew he was making the right choice.

He just hoped Shawna felt the same way.

Sometimes he got the feeling Shawna knew what he was planning. The canoe trip had been his idea—an intimate, three-day excursion that would take them through several bodies of water and across some forty miles of untouched wilderness. While planning the long weekend, he'd researched less-traveled rivers, selecting rural, southern countryside most people had never heard of. That was the whole point—privacy and the beauty of nature, two things they never got back home in D.C.

"Isn't it gorgeous here?" Paul asked.

Shawna nodded and looked out from the bank, admiring the calm river cutting through the clusters of limestone, carrying dead leaves on its murky surface. Autumn was crumbling into winter, and the trees were spindly, the bark gone pale.

"Not as gorgeous as you, though," Paul told his girlfriend.

She rolled her eyes but smiled. "Yeah, yeah."

Paul meant what he'd said. Shawna was a lovely brunette just past her twenty-seventh birthday, with chestnut eyes and wide hips. Paul was only two years older but had always felt she was out of his league. He'd never had a girlfriend that looked this good. But looks weren't everything.

Shawna was also smart and creative, with good taste in music and a great sense of humor. Even his mother, who'd always thought Paul's girlfriends were never good enough for him, loved Shawna, as did the rest of Paul's family. It was as if she'd been tailor made just for him.

"So," she said, "are you ready to get back on the water?"

Paul bit his bottom lip. "In a minute."

He took her hand, and she sat beside him on the fallen tree, nuzzling into him. He kissed the top of her head.

"It really is nice out here," she said. "So peaceful."

"It's great to get away from the noise of the city."

"What area are we in now?"

"Not sure. This is the Hollow River, but I don't know what this place is called, if it's even incorporated land."

"Middle of nowhere is fine by me," she said, slipping her arms around his waist. "This way I get you all to myself."

How'd you like to have me all to yourself for the rest of your life? Paul thought.

Was now the right time? He wanted to create a cherished memory. Maybe he should wait for sunset or even a sunrise, but the days were growing gloomier with winter coming, and he couldn't guarantee they'd see either. The anxiousness was also killing him. The sooner he asked her, the sooner his nerves would settle, and then, if she said yes, he could enjoy the canoe trip even more.

"Babe…" he began.

She looked up at him, and in those soft, brown eyes Paul saw his future. It looked absolutely perfect. Sneaking, he reached for the zipper on his backpack.

Paul cleared his throat. "I wanna, um… I wanna ask you someth—"

The sound of snapping twigs caused Paul to stop mid-sentence. The noise was growing louder, the footsteps nearer. He and Shawna turned to look, and when they spotted a lumbering figure between the sparse trees, Paul stood, feeling Shawna tug on his wrist as if telling him to sit back down, though he wasn't sure why.

"Shit," he whispered to her. "Hope this isn't private land."

Shawna didn't reply. She was staring at the man coming down the pathway. He was wide-shouldered, heavyset, with graying hair and a weathered face hidden in shadow. His denim jacket clashed with his slacks, which looked more like pajama bottoms than proper pants. Something about the guy made Paul uneasy. If he were a fisherman or lumberjack, where was his gear? He was deep in the woods alone with no hiking pack or other equipment. Not even a dog. It rose a lot of questions.

Shawna stood up too, her backpack in hand. "Babe, we should go."

"You think so?"

"What if this is his property? He might not be welcoming to trespassers."

"But if we take off, that'll make us look guilty of something. We're just making a pit-stop. No big deal."

"Not to us, but…"

Paul looked to his girlfriend—hopefully his fiancé by the end of the day—and decided whatever she wanted to do was best. He gathered his backpack and canteen just as the stranger came down to the bank.

"Howdy," the big man said.

Now Paul saw his face. It was gray in the pale, November daylight. There was a scar on the man's neck the size of a quarter. There was something familiar about the mountain man, but instead of that putting Paul at ease, it only made him more nervous. Though he couldn't place the stranger, the familiarity brought a quiet dread.

"We were just leaving," Paul blurted out.

The mountain man grinned with horrible teeth. "On a little journey, are ya?"

"Yeah," he said, putting the backpack over his shoulders. "Headed upriver."

Paul could feel Shawna pulling away, urging him toward their canoe. She remained silent even as the mountain man turned his black eyes on her, looking her up and down as if selecting a cut of meat.

"This your darlin'?" he asked Paul while keeping his gaze on Shawna.

Though it was a chilly afternoon, Paul began to sweat. Shawna tugged his sleeve again.

"Listen," Paul said, sounding weaker than he'd like to. "We really have to get going—"

The mountain man took a step forward, singing under his breath. "*Oh, my darlin', Clementine. You are lost and gone forever. Dreadful sorrow, Clementine.*"

Shawna pulled harder and started down to the shore. Paul followed her, both moving as quickly as they could without breaking into a run. The mountain man pursued them, still serenading them, his ominous baritone growing louder.

"*Hit her soft head with a boulder, fell into the foamin' brine... ruby lips above the water, blowin' bubbles soft 'n fine...*"

Paul ushered Shawna into the canoe. Her lovely eyes were now dark with worry. Seeing the fear in her sent a mean heat through him. If he couldn't protect her, how could he have the nerve to ask for her hand in marriage? He turned around to the face the creep, determined to make a stand.

"You need to back off," Paul said, pointing at him.

For his size, the mountain man moved swiftly, his hand going behind his back and returning with a knife. Paul's mouth went dry. It wasn't a pocketknife or hunting knife the man held. It was a kitchen knife—a *butcher* knife—crusted with what looked like dried blood.

Paul doubted the man had been skinning a deer. He put up his hands passively, hoping to reason with the stranger, but as the man lunged Paul realized where he recognized him from, and knew then there would be no reasoning, no bargaining, and no escape.

"Shawna!" he cried, not so she would come to his aid but so she would take this opportunity to paddle away while Paul tried to fight the stranger off.

Only he wasn't a stranger anymore. He was too famous for that.

And soon, Paul would be famous too.

***

Blood shot out of the young man's belly, warming Edmund's hand as he thrust the blade in and out, stabbing him a dozen times in a matter of seconds. Though his victim tried to defend himself, he was just a skinny city boy from a sissy generation. Probably had never been in a fight in his life. Edmund twisted the blade and then ripped it out sideways, the young man's belly opening in a wet pop. All the while the girl called Shawna shrieked and cried, stirring Edmund's loins as he shoved the young man to the dirt.

To Edmund's surprise, Shawna tried to rescue her beau. She came up from the canoe swinging an oar but was no more skilled in battle than her boyfriend. Edmund dodged her attack with ease, and as the oar whipped past, Shawna lost her balance. Edmund grabbed her by the hair, breaking her fall but kicking her in the belly, causing her to drop the oar. Shawna groaned as her air escaped her, a soft sigh like an orgasm gone sour. Edmund sucked his teeth. He pulled Shawna's hair, forcing her head back and knocking her to her knees, which was exactly where a pretty, young thing like her belonged.

"You're a hell of a woman," he said.

She shut her eyes tight. Heavy gasps caused her chest to rise and fall, and Edmund imagined what her breasts must look like

35

under that flannel, and what they were going to look like torn from her ribcage. He waited for Shawna to plead for her life, but she only trembled. That was alright. They all begged eventually. That's when the bargaining would be begin, a fun little game they always lost.

"*Oh, my darlin'…*" Edmund sang.

He ran the blade down Shawna's cheek, not breaking the skin but allowing her boyfriend's blood to dribble down her face.

"*Oh, my darlin'…*"

She shivered, a soaking wet dog on a winter's day. He pressed the tip of the blade just under her right eye.

"*Oh, my darlin', Clementine.*"

Edmund pressed a little harder, digging into Shawna's bottom eyelid. He recalled the book of Matthew from the scripture they had forced him to hear as a child, all that religious poetry spouted from a mad preacher.

"*If thy right eye offends thee,*" Edmund quoted, "*pluck it out and cast it from thee.*"

His new darling tried to fight him, but he was far stronger and more determined to cause pain than she was to avoid it. She screamed, but with no one else around to hear her, it was a beautiful love song just for him, and though she pleaded for her life, Edmund knew what was best for her, what was best for them both.

EIGHT

"JESUS FUCKING CHRIST," Keith said, putting the photo on top of the others and closing the manila folder.

He'd seen what Edmund Cox was capable of before, having examined fresh crime scenes in the madman's wake, but could never get used to the level of brutality inflicted upon the victims. Even the aftermath of the carnage was an assault, Edmund leaving behind human remains so grotesque they lingered long in memory.

Across the table from Keith, Darius Clay reached for the folder, putting it aside. Hooded eyes reflected his exhaustion. Given the urgency of the manhunt, Keith could imagine the long hours his partner must have been pulling.

"I can't believe it," Keith said. "How the hell did he get *two* of his groupies in the same place?"

Darius sighed. "We don't know. It was Lori's apartment. At first, we thought the other body belonged to her sister, because they lived together. Instead, it belonged to Niko Hayashi. Even though she was Asian and Lori was white, they were so mutilated it was hard to tell them apart. It was like putting two jigsaw puzzles back together at the same time."

"I swear," Keith said, tapping his beer with his fingernails. "Those two bitches were almost as sick as he was."

"Almost."

"I hate to say it, but they asked for this. I'm not saying they had it coming, but…"

"They should've expected nothing less of Edmund Cox."

"Exactly." Keith finished the bottle. "He certainly wasted no time coming to see them. You think they knew he was getting out? Maybe they helped him somehow?"

"I don't see how they could have."

They didn't bother rehashing the details of the prison. They were both caught up on Edmund's escape now, Darius holding nothing back as he'd given Keith all the updates he'd missed while on leave. Keith was grateful for his partner's time. He knew how valuable it was, but after seeing that news report on TV, he had to know more.

"What about Lori's sister? Abby, right?"

Darius nodded. "She's missing. There's some concern that Cox may have taken her hostage—"

"Edmund Cox doesn't take hostages."

"I agree. If we ever find that woman, she'll just be a body."

"I wish they'd let me come back," Keith said in a huff. "I should be on this case. I studied this sick fuck for years. You and I know more about Cox than most of those dildos they've got on it now."

"The F.B.I is all over it."

"Fuck the F.B.I. If they were smart, they'd have come talk to me after Cox escaped. They'd get me back on duty so I could find the bastard for them."

Darius shrugged. "I don't know if that's up to them, but they're in charge now."

"A lot of good they're doing. Cox has already taken two more lives since he busted out. Two that we know of, but probably three with the sister. And there's probably even more. You know how insatiable his bloodlust is. He doesn't cool off between murders the way most serial killers do. With him, the havoc never stops."

"He's on the move again," Darius said. "Just like he was before we caught him the first time. He stole one of the victim's cars when he fled the scene and they still haven't been able to locate it, let alone him."

"What about you? Where do you think he's gone?"

"Shit, man. Who the hell knows?" Darius took a deep breath. "We've combed through his old stomping grounds, but he had so damned many of them. He took residence in a lot of different towns and left bodies in multiple states. But the feds think Cox isn't going to return to any of them, anyway. They think he's too smart for that, that he'll know we'll be looking for him in those places. That's why they've pulled their men back."

"What?" Keith asked, surprised. "Already?"

"The people in charge have directed the searches elsewhere now. Don't ask me what leads they're following instead." He shrugged. "They're playing things close to the chest now, so there's a good deal of classified information I'm not privy too. Being in the dark, a lot of what they're doing doesn't make sense to me."

As night fell, they had another round, and the conversation shifted to personal matters, Darius asking how Keith's sessions with the shrink were going but neither of them bringing up the Josh Negus shooting. Keith insisted on paying the bar tab, and his partner told him he'd keep him in the loop about the manhunt, but Darius couldn't promise much now that the feds were orchestrating every move—*and therefore committing every fuck up.* Whatever information they had would stay out of Keith's reach, but that didn't mean it was the only information out there. One just had to know where to look, and Keith had a pretty good idea.

Though he'd had four beers, he was far from drunk, and wasn't about to let his blood alcohol level stop him. He lit a cigarette, climbed into his car, and drove toward the highway, heading south.

NINE

THE MUSIC WAS HYPNOTIC, an otherworldly cyclone of sound unlike any Gary had heard before. The songs were not repetitive rip-offs of the hook in Muddy Waters' "Mannish Boy", as many blues songs were, but rich originals with wandering guitars and ghostly vocals, telling stories of heartbreak, lust, and violent crime. Junior's juke joint wasn't as lively as it was on weekends, but several patrons were gyrating on the small dance floor before the even smaller stage where an elderly black man sang upon a stool, fingering his electric guitar. Two younger men flanked the bluesman, one on bass and the other behind a weathered drum set. An open guitar case was sprinkled with dollars and quarters.

Magic marker on a shred of cardboard made for a sign.

"*Lightnin' Booba Barlow*," it read.

Gary scanned the place from his barstool. It was a southern dive bar made more interesting by live music and a rustic atmosphere that made him feel as if he'd taken several steps backward through time. Everything was outdated. The sparse lightbulbs gave off a sickly yellow glow, revealing a cigarette machine and a '50s-style jukebox. Someone had coated barstools with electrical tape to seal rips. There was a kitchen in the back, and the smell of chicken-fried steak, chili sauce, and fried okra stirred

Gary's appetite.

"You good?" the barman asked, pointing at Gary's empty glass of lemonade. "Wanna refill?"

Gary nodded. The barman was in his early fifties, his hair grown out and wiry. Gary thought he looked like Jesse Jackson. The barman refilled his glass and wiped the spillover off the bar with a rag gone gray from frequent use and infrequent washes. Gary dropped a five-dollar bill before him.

"Refills is free," the barman said, "less'un you want alcyhol".

"Nah. That's for you."

The barman tucked the bill in the pouch of his apron. "Much obliged."

Gary hoped for a quick return on his investment. "I was wondering if I could ask you a few things."

The barman's face changed. He seemed guarded already, a discouragement to any investigator.

"Oh?" the barman said, the smile fading to blankness.

Gary proceeded anyway. "I'm new in town and—"

"Shit, man. You really thinks you needa tell me that?"

Gary smirked. He supposed that was fair enough. In small communities like Killen, everyone tended to know each other. Even the hermits of the woods had to come to town for supplies. Gary also stood out in his gray slacks and blazer, new shoes, and button-up shirt. Many of the men around here probably didn't wear shirts at all in the warmer months.

Now that the cold season had rolled in, they wore flannels under their overalls, not casual suits. Gary was a clean cut, modern man. Black or white, the residents of Killen were all hillbillies and mountain folk—human relics of a lost age, as if they'd been ripped from the pages of Cormac McCarthy and Toni Morrison novels.

"I'm only visiting," Gary said. "I'm here looking for someone. A friend."

"Ain't seen no new faces 'round here, other than yours."

"Well, how about a few months ago? My friend would've stood out even more than me."

He drew a picture of Jessica Hong from his blazer's pocket.

In the photo, she was in a billowy sweater, standing before a garden of bougainvillea. Her smile was bright as a star, one Gary feared had gone out.

The barman gave the photo a passing glance. "Can't help ya, mister."

"Look, I'm not a cop, if that's what you're worried about. Are you sure you don't want to take a closer—"

"I done said I ain't seen 'er."

"You're sure?"

"I'da remembered a Japanese."

"Chinese," Gary corrected. "Her name is Hong. Jessica Hong."

The barman shook his head, implying Gary didn't listen very well. He started wiping down the entire bar, an excuse to walk away.

"Listen," Gary said. "I have reason to believe this girl was a victim of Edmund Cox."

The bartender froze, and time seemed to freeze along with him. "We don't talk 'bout him in these parts."

"I'm just trying to find—"

"*I said* we don't talk 'bout him. Not never."

Gary knew better than to press, so he changed the subject as the barman turned away. "How about the River Man?"

The barman went rigid, his face harder and grayer. He stood up straight, shifting his jaw as if chewing tobacco.

"Whatchu doin' comin' in here talkin' 'bout all this?" he asked.

"My friend," Gary said. "She was studying southern folklore. She wrote a paper on hillside blues music, and another on the legend of The River Man."

"Shit." The barman smiled sardonically. "I dunno nothin' 'bout no tall tales, mister. I just serve the drinks, m'kay?"

But Gary didn't believe him. The man's nervousness revealed what he was trying to conceal. Detective's intuition told Gary the ghost story of this River Man character had something to do with Edmund Cox, however small. Wouldn't such a dark legend have some influence over a serial killer who was born here?

Gary put another five on the bar. "C'mon. What's the harm if it's just a legend?"

The barman eyed the bill, then gave Gary a stare before snatching it up. He looked both ways like an informant snitching to the police.

"There's more harm to askin' 'bout River Man than you can even imagine," he said in a low tone. "Best advice I can give ya is to get the hell outta here."

Gary lowered his brow. "You throwin' me out?"

"I mean get the hell outta Killen. Ya don't wanna go 'round askin' no questions. Not here, mister. Specially not 'bout that ol' wives' tale."

The barman's last nerve seemed taut. Recognizing this, Gary thanked him for his time and strolled about the juke joint, watching Lightnin' Booba Barlow's fingers move upon the guitar as quickly as his nickname. Gary observed the patrons moving amongst the shadows like wraiths. A black woman swayed her generous hips, hands in the air and snapping her fingers. She looked about Gary's age and was adorned in a faded sundress and no shoes, the pink polish on her toenails chipped, her calves muscular.

When the song ended, Booba paused for a shot of whiskey, and Gary moseyed over to the woman. He was about to ask her the same questions he'd asked the bartender, but a large, white man with tattooed anacondas for arms moved in on her first. She smiled as he put his arm around her. When the man's hard eyes fell upon Gary, he moved on, and this time when he scanned the room, he felt many eyes on him.

Stranger in a strange land, he thought.

Killen was about as welcoming as a razor wire fence.

Booba and the band started in on another tune. The lyrics sent Gary's neck hairs on end.

"*That ol' man on the river, baby,*" Booba sang. "*I'm goin' to his mountain home. River Man gonna greet me, gonna bring me women 'n gold. When you head on down his river, baby, better offer up your soul.*"

The spindly musician tore into the guitar in the style of heavy metal, though the band remained in a blues rhythm. The rest of the lyrics hinted at the things Gary had read about in Jessica Hong's essay—a mythic, eremitical man in a Killen river shack who grants wishes at a terrible cost, a sort of human version of a monkey's paw. It was a Faustian tale. Some called The River Man a ghost. Others swore he was a wayward demon or an agent of Satan. Though the bartender implied people were tightlipped when it came to local legend, the tradition of using song to express the forbidden was as old as music itself.

Booba's band closed with a cover of John Lee Hooker's "Burnin' Hell," then came down the steps and proceeded to the bar. Gary started after them but noticed the barman watching him with a mean glint in his eye. After that song about The River Man, the bartender knew damned well what Gary was after. He made a hand signal and a black man even larger than the guy with the anaconda arms emerged from the corner with nostrils flared. Gary headed toward the exit, but that wasn't good enough for the bouncer. He pursued Gary like a predator, and just as Gary opened the door the bouncer grabbed hold of his collar and shoved him against the doorjamb.

"You stay outta here!" the bouncer said. "You come 'round here again and you gonna wish your cracker ass ain't never been born."

Shoved through the doorway, Gary stumbled in the loose gravel of the lot. He hid a pistol in an ankle holster, but never pulled it unless he intended to use it. He straightened his blazer, looking back at the bouncer but saying nothing. The bouncer slammed the door behind him. Gary took a deep breath. It wasn't the first time someone had thrown him out of a place, but it remained an experience he could do without.

He walked to his car and drove a short distance away, parked, and took his binoculars from his travel case. It was time to test the virtue of patience.

It was almost an hour before Booba came outside. A rusty van from the 1980s pulled to the side of the juke joint, the younger band members loading their equipment while the old man leaned on his cane. Gary got out of his car and returned to the juke joint's parking lot.

Booba lit an unfiltered cigarette. His porkpie hat was the perfect topper for his ensemble of flannel shirt, suspenders, and slacks with patches on the knees. Those enormous, wrap-around sunglasses old people wore hid half his face, a white soul patch below his bottom lip.

Gary gave him a friendly wave. "Mr. Barlow?"

The bluesman nodded. "Booba, son."

"Okay, Booba. I'm Gary Chatmon. Just wanted to say that was an amazing show."

"Thank ya kindly. We do 'preciate it."

"You play a guitar like you're ringin' a bell," Gary said with snicker. "Just like that old song says."

"That be Chuck Berry."

"Yeah, that's it. I really enjoyed your lyrics too. They're like poetry. I especially liked that one about the man on the river."

Gary waited for Booba to go rigid like the bartender had, but if the bluesman did, it was undetectable. His skeletal frame was already rigid, and the dark lenses of his glasses concealed his eyes.

"Well," Booba said. "I's can't take credit for that one. That's but a spin on a local oldie."

"Oh, really? It's a traditional song?"

Booba blew smoke. "Not as such. It were written by a man named Jackson Fledderjohn, some seventy years ago, I reckon."

"Was he from around here?"

"Yep. Think his son still lives down the river. Name of Buzz. Jackson Fledderjohn was a big name in these parts for a short while."

"A successful musician?"

"For a spell." Booba shook his head. "But he done threw it all away. Killed a man. Murdered his own wife too—with a fryin' pan, if I recall. Maybe he done killed more. It's been so long now. I'm older than the moon, so my memory can't be trusted none."

"The man he was singing about—The River Man. That's a local legend, right?"

A plume of smoke rose from the old man's throat. He was silent, as if choosing his next words carefully.

"Yeah," he said. "River Man be a campfire story. Ghost tales."

"That bartender got really uptight when I mentioned it. Why would he get so mad over a ghost story?"

Booba puffed, taking his time. "Prolly 'cause a lotta folks say it *ain't* just a story. Killen has a history as bloody as a battlefield. Folks say it's cursed earth. Sinners need somebody to blame for the wicked things they done, so they create a devil. Our devil be The River Man."

Encouraged, Gary reached into his coat. "I know a young woman who wrote all about this. Would you mind looking at her photo? She's been missing and—"

Booba raised a hand to stop Gary. "Can't look at nothin' for ya, son." The bluesman removed his sunglasses. His eyes were white from cataracts, one eyelid half-closed. Thin scars were etched across the flesh surrounding the sockets. "Been blind since the days of Jimmy Carter."

"Oh," Gary said, putting the picture away. "I'm sorry, I didn't know."

"S'all right. God done gimmie other gifts."

"You are one hell of a musician. I'll bet you'd give that Jackson Fledderjohn a run for his money."

Booba's alabaster eyes locked on Gary's then, as if defying their blindness. "Nah. Ol' Jackson done made a deal, so they say. If Idda gone down the same path as him, Idda seen the same fate as that poor soul."

"Deal?" Gary's eyebrows drew closer together. "You mean a deal with The River Man?"

Booba put his glasses back on, saying nothing.

"Thought you said that was only a ghost story," Gary said.

"It is."

A stiff wind picked up, the dark clouds promising freezing rain. The bass player closed the van door and, spotting Gary, started toward them.

His gaze was stern, telling Gary he recognized him as the

man who'd been tossed out, so Gary wrapped things up with Booba before the situation became hostile.

"Well," he said. "I thank you for—"

"Don't go lookin', son," Booba said, cutting Gary off. "Best advice I ever got, and now Imma give it to you—a man who keeps diggin' is a man who digs his own grave."

The words chilled Gary more than the November breeze.

"Thanks for your time," he said. He noted the small, gold cross hanging for Booba's necklace, and though Gary was an atheist, he said, "God bless you, Booba."

The old man flashed a yellow smile. "Oh, he has. *He has.*"

TEN

THE REMNANTS OF THE DEAD cotton fields seemed to shiver in the rising breeze. Encroaching clouds moved in heather plumes across the stratosphere like a herd of bison driving down from the mountains. Distant thunder groaned, the sound echoing off the walls of the gorge and vibrating the black stone, but the threat of rain didn't deter June from entering the woods. Nothing would. As she descended the hill, wind whistled through the hollow like lonesome whale songs. She heard no critters or insects, no signs of life. The only movement was fallen leaves fluttering along the trail and the gentle trembling of tree limbs.

Though she'd grown up in Killen, she'd never been this deep in the woods before. They warned children to stay away from this part of the river, and to never approach the shacks that were peppered throughout the thicket like memorials for a simpler yet darker time.

"Promise me you'll never go down there," June's grandmother had once said.

June had agreed back then, but she wasn't five anymore, and Gramma was dead. That was the nature of this shit-ass river town. It sowed suffering and reaped blood harvests. Even those who escaped murder and suicide found their way to an early pauper's grave. June had considered visiting her grandmother's grave, which was little more than a death certificate on a plaque the size of a paperback book, but couldn't face Gramma again, not even with six feet of cemetery dirt between them.

Though this was June's big return home, she tried to keep her thoughts off her old family. Instead, she thought about the man she'd long wanted in her life. She'd watched him in all the interviews and had listened to the released recordings of his interrogations. She'd read a dense true crime book about him and listened to multiple podcasts that covered his story.

The life and crimes of Edmund Cox, she thought as she hefted the weight of the magazines and newspapers in her backpack. She'd stuffed them in there along with the few personal items she owned. June didn't have much for camping gear, but she'd spent so many nights sleeping under bridges and inside condemned buildings that it hardly mattered. She was a vagabond veteran and could make a nest wherever she ended up.

Edmund Cox was a roamer too. Like June, he'd come from this cursed land. Killen was as close to the idea of home as either of them would ever have. There was a certain kinship in that, however toxic. It was good to know they had some things in common. Maybe it would make this easier.

June followed the trail as it wound downhill. She felt as if she were disassociating, entering a world outside the one she'd always known. Though Killen was her old hometown, she was treading on unfamiliar soil. It reminded her of her first adventures in the west, when she'd seen the dunes of Arizona and the psychedelic canyon rock of Nevada. It had seemed like another planet. While these woods weren't as alien, a tombstone-gray hue tainted the surrounding wilderness, making everything look more like a charcoal drawing. All was drab and dead and without hope. Even the rushing water at the banks below seemed somehow empty. Maybe that's why they called it the Hollow River. It churned, dark and nebulous, an aquatic void impenetrable by light.

She was heading toward it when she saw him.

June tucked herself behind a pine and looked down at the man walking along the riverbank. He was tall and spindly, his arms so long they appeared out of proportion with his body. A withered, black suit hung upon him like sacks, and a country gentleman's hat sat askew upon his gnarly head, hiding the top half of his face. She could only see his rictus grin and the sickly, tissue paper flesh. But while his appearance was off-putting, it was his behavior that kept June hidden behind the tree.

The old man was signing in a high and fluttery voice, sounding more like a choir boy than a geriatric. *"When I hear them trumpets sound, Imma rise up outta the ground. Ain't no grave, can hold my body down."*

He clutched his hands together. June stared at what appeared to be long, boneless fingers. Looking more closely, she saw one of them tilt upwards, and a small, forked tongue flickered out.

June's breath caught in her chest.

Snakes, she realized.

As the old man drew closer—still unaware of June's presence—she got a better look at the serpents coiled around his arms and cradled in his hands. Some were harmless garden snakes. Others were the kind June's grandmother had taught her to stay away from—copperheads, water moccasins, and coral snakes. Though she didn't see any diamondbacks, she heard the distinct rattle. It seemed to chime in rhythm with the man's song.

The old man stopped and raised his bundle of serpents toward the churning heavens, as if offering them to some dark deity.

"Well, meet me, Jesus, meet me," he sang. *"Catch me in the middle of the air. Cause if these wings done fail me, God won't gimmie another pair."*

When he turned his head toward the sky, the shadow across his eyes lifted, and June saw his face in all its grotesquery. His cheeks were sallow, the blotchy flesh draped over his skull like wet satin. She'd never seen a more pronounced skull on a living human being. His eyes were cavernous and jaundiced, his teeth like broken glass. As he reached toward the thunderclouds, his sleeves dropped to his elbows, revealing a litany of bite marks that covered his skin like spots on a cheetah's coat.

He continued to serenade.

"Look way down his river, and whatta ya think I see? I see The Devil's legion, and they're comin' after me."

He repositioned the snakes on his right arm, draping them over his neck like scarves, and reached into his coat, drawing out a small Mason jar. Gripping the neck of the water moccasin, he pinched it, agitating it enough so its mouth opened wide in a hiss. The old man snickered and pressed the snake's fangs against the rim of the Mason jar. Venom poured from the water moccasin's jaws, collecting in the jar's bottom. He eased the pressure on the riled snake, and once it relaxed, the old man raised the jar to his mouth and knocked back the venom as if it were a shot of whiskey. He smacked his lips, the copperheads coiling around his neck like nooses.

Everything felt suddenly colder. June hugged herself as the snake-handler put the jar back in his coat and started walking down the bank again, his skeletal body lumbering like a cornfield scarecrow brought to life. She remained hidden as he moved on, sticking to the riverbank instead of crossing her on the trail. There was a sour odor on the breeze now, a smell like dumpsters in August, like human remains baking under the sun. June couldn't be sure if the stink belonged to the old man, but it left with him. The last trace of him was his fluttery vocals as he sang into the twisted woods of Killen.

"Well, I'm goin' down his river. Bury my knees in the sand. Gonna holler high 'Hosanna', 'til I reach that River Man."

ELEVEN

FINISHED WITH HER, Edmund searched Shawna's belongings, then went on to the young man's backpack. Most of it was useless to him, all the trinkets and gadgets the modern world had grown too dependent on, phones and other do-dads a man of his ilk deemed unnecessary. They were the tools of the weak. A real man had no need for a global positioning system; he followed the stars. Real men had no use for video games, headphones, or text messages. They were mere toys. These things were the essence of softness, of weakness, of little boys walking around in the flabby husks of an adult body. Edmund was too well-bred for such juvenile tripe. He chose the tools of the strong—hammers, zip ties, axes, rope. His latest victims had none, but their backpacks had pull-strings, so Edmund cut them free with his butcher knife.

He drew the blood-crusted wad of paper from his pocket, letting his treasures breathe. Niko's teeth rolled in his bare hand like peppercorns. Lori's finger was curled with the early stages of decay, but her eye remained bright and moist, as if still alive.

Look upon me, darlin', he thought, speaking with his heart. *Look upon me and our world. I'm takin' you with me all the way, baby girl. We're comin' home.*

He placed his keepsakes on the ground and returned to

Shawna's slack body. Edmund smiled at a job well done. It was amazing what a simple kitchen knife could do, the way it could transform a human being, stripping away the beauty of the flesh to reveal the rotten core within. Taking Shawna's bottom lip between two fingers, he stretched the meat taut so the blade could catch it better. He began to saw. Blood sprinkled across Shawna's corpse and spattered upon the expunged teeth resting in her lap, the debris of spent passions.

Placing the severed lip in the wad of paper with his other treasures, he cut one of the pull strings in half and tied Shawna's lip to Lori's finger. He shoved Niko's teeth between the two, sandwiching the chipped molars in strips of female meat. Edmund had no use for the remains of the young man. He'd been a necessary kill, not one of Edmund's darlings. He'd never shied away from taking a man's life, but while it offered a cheap thrill, it was not his objective. Mutilation was an intimate act, same as making love, and he penetrated women's bodies with a wide variety of tools, not just the one nature had graced him with.

Using the other half of the string, Edmund tightened the wad of human remains into a straight shaft, uncurling Lori's finger and aligning Niko's teeth so they wedged deep into the pulp of Shawna's lower lip. He left Lori's eye separate from this mass. He cradled it in his palm again, so she could better see his handywork.

Just a work in progress, darlin'. Don't worry none. We'll find all the parts we need, all the pieces of his puzzle.

Grabbing one of Shawna's spare shirts, he wiped the young couple's blood from the butcher knife and tucked it back through his belt like a saber. Other than her lip and the strings, the only item he took from them was Shawne's panties, which she'd soiled when Edmund had started on her. He gave them a quick sniff, then rolled them into a ball and stuffed them into one pocket, the wad of human remains into the other, and continued his quest.

TWELVE

KEITH DIDN'T RECEIVE A WARM WELCOME, but cops rarely did in poor communities like Killen. Though he wore plain clothes, the hicks easily sniffed out the law when it came creeping through their town. Asking questions here was asking for trouble. He knew that. But Keith Drakeson had never responded well to the word "no." The people he'd busted during his career would attest to that, even the ones he'd let go. So, when the waitress brought him his lunch, he started in with his queries, asking if she knew anything about Edmund Cox.

"You must be with that other feller," she said. "I already done told him all I know."

"Other fellow?"

"That detective lookin' for the missin' girl." The waitress narrowed her gaze. "Ain't you with him?"

"Yeah," Keith said. "You happen to know where he went?"

The waitress shifted uncomfortably. "Listen, I don't wanna get caught in the middle of no—"

She shut her mouth when he put a twenty on the table.

"You've lived here all your life," Keith told her as they locked eyes. "Let me guess. You got pregnant young and the guy who knocked you up went out for cigarettes and never came back. And I'm guessing you have more than one baby to feed now.

So, you work your ass off in this place, sweating and putting up with whiny customers, all to come home with a bad back and barely enough of a paycheck to pay the rent."

The waitress' jaw went tight, lips sealed. In her eyes, Keith saw all the confirmation he needed.

"You need this money," he said, "and I need to know where my friend went. A tip for a tip. That's all."

She took a deep breath, squinting at Keith, then slid the bill from the table.

After eating, Keith walked to The Sunshine Motel. No one answered the first two doors he knocked on. An ancient maid with an eyepatch was cleaning the third room. Keith hoped he hadn't missed his mystery man. He passed by the room with the missing door and knocked on another. He heard shuffling behind it and his hand instinctively went to his hip to be closer to his holstered pistol.

"Who is it?" a male voice asked from behind the door.

"Police," Keith said.

A pause, then, "what is this about?"

"Can you open the door please, sir?"

Another pause, and then the door came open, revealing a middle-aged man in his undershirt and slacks. A twenty-four-hour news network was on the TV, and there was an open laptop on the table, papers fanned about it like playing cards.

"Can I see a badge?" the man asked.

Keith drew his billfold from his pocket, flashing his shield.

"Now you," Keith said. "Let me see your credentials."

"Tell me what this is about first."

"Sir—"

"This ain't Nazi Germany. I don't have to give you I.D on command unless you suspect me of a crime. Now do you?"

"Easy, pal." Keith put up his hands in a passive manner. "No need to call the ACLU. I just want to talk to you."

"About what?"

Keith lowered his brow. "About Edmund Cox."

They stared at each other, neither looking away. The man opened the door and stepped back, allowing Keith inside, then closed it behind him.

"Okay," the man said. "Ask."

"Who are you?"

"Gary Chatmon. Private investigator. Who're you?"

"Detective Keith Drakeson. What's a private investigator doing hunting an escaped serial killer?"

"I'm not. This is just a missing person's job." Gary explained the case, then asked, "How did you know I was here?"

"You're not the only one who can get answers out of people. Throw these rednecks a couple of bucks and they'll rat out their own mothers." He looked around the room with a keen eye. "I gotta tell ya, Chatmon. If a young girl went missing around here, I wouldn't hold out much hope of finding her alive, especially if she was Asian. You're probably wasting your time."

"Try telling that to her family," Gary said, crossing his arms.

Keith narrowed his eyes. "Why're you so hostile against cops?"

"Not hostile, just cautious."

"You ever work on the force?"

"Nah. I'm a private dick, not a public one."

Keith let the jab slide. "I was on the task force that caught Cox. Son of a bitch didn't stay caught long though. They should've executed him while they had the chance. Instead, he's on the loose again."

"That's why you're in Killen then? I expected there to be more of you guys around."

"Well, I'm the lead investigator."

"Seems to me you'd have a partner—hell, a whole SWAT team, considering what you're up against."

"I do things my own way. I found Cox before—I'll find him again."

Gary smirked. "I see. So, what is this then? Some personal vendetta? Dirty Harry out to catch the Zodiac Killer by any means necessary?"

"Edmund Cox is a psychotic killer. I'm trying to keep him from taking any more of these Chinese girls away from their families. Sorry if that takes business away from you."

Gary's smirk faded. He stared out the window, gentle rain pelting the glass. "Okay. So, you're looking for Cox. I'm not. I'm not trying to take any glory away from you boys in blue and sure as shit don't want to confront that maniac. That's nowhere in my job description. I'm just following the information I have in the hopes of giving a suffering family some semblance of closure."

Keith nodded.

"So where does that leave us?" Gary asked.

Keith rubbed his chin. "Maybe we could help each other."

"You serious?"

"You said you're following information," Keith said, pointing at the laptop and papers. "I'd like to know just what you have."

Gary seemed to consider this. "Are you saying you'll give me access to police files in return?"

"Hell no. But I will answer any questions you have, provided they aren't classified."

"Seems I could get that from newspapers."

"You'll get more than the press does. It might be just what you need to find the Hong girl. Or her body, at least."

Gary sighed. He looked to the table where his laptop sat open, then offered a weak smile.

"Okay, detective," he said. He turned the computer so the screen faced Keith. "Right now, I'm researching local folklore. A ghost story, of all things." He laughed at himself. "Probably seems silly to you, but—"

"There's nothing silly about The River Man," Keith said.

Gary froze, his face falling slack.

"Cox talked about him often," Keith said. "Of course, it was in his usual, nonsensical way of speaking. He was just like Charles Manson in that regard, his confessions like song lyrics. But that little ghost story was always on his mind."

Gary nodded. "I thought he might know of it. Seemed too morbid for a man like him to not take interest."

"Oh, it was more than a passing interest. Cox was obsessed with it—that and ripping young ladies apart." He stepped closer to Gary. "My question to you is… how did *you* know about it?"

"I'm a good private investigator. Besides, Jessica Hong was a student of folklore. She wrote a paper about this River Man legend. I think her interest in the subject is what brought her here. Everyone in this town gets tightlipped when you bring the legend up, just as they do when you bring up Cox. It's enough to make me believe there's some fact to the story, however small."

"Most urban legends start with truths," Keith said. "They just get more fantastical as the story is passed from person to person. It's like the telephone game. Everyone adds their own flourish to the tale when they retell it. Same reason we separate suspects when we question them."

Gary's face turned grim. "I think there's something on this river. And I think it has something to do with the people we're looking for."

"And you might just be right."

Gary took a deep breath, hands on his hips again. "Okay then. Let's do it."

THIRTEEN

THE GENTLE RAIN REMINDED JUNE of the long car ride to Huntersville Glenn. Her grandparents had always tried to make it easier on her, letting her pick out candy and a comic book at the drugstore before leaving town, but no number of amenities had ever been enough to quench her unease. Knowing where they were going—and what awaited them—had always made the journey a slog of dread. Even the sky must have sensed it, for it seemed to rain every time they went to the asylum.

Grandpa always went inside first while June and her grandmother waited in the car. This was to keep young June from seeing anything she shouldn't. Often the waiting room was filled with unwell people about to be committed, sometimes against their will. After signing in, Grandpa would come back to the car and the three of them would make their way inside. It was a large building, gray as a tombstone. June could still remember the smell—a sour aroma of riboflavin, urine, and mothballs. An orderly would escort them to a visiting room where pale fluorescents flickered overhead, and then they would be left alone, giving them one last moment to brace themselves as a family before the horror would start again.

No matter how many times her grandparents told June the madwoman was her mother, she could never really believe it.

They shared the same long, dark hair and pale complexion, but otherwise, they couldn't have been more different. June was a fresh-faced little girl then. Her so-called mother was human wreckage, so lost in the cobwebs of insanity it seemed pointless to even make these visits. She mostly just hung her head, using her hair as a divider, a shield against socializing even with her own family. June was grateful for that curtain of hair, for whenever she glimpsed her mother's face it caused her nightmares. She was so horribly disfigured it pained everyone to look at her. It was a crushing reminder of everything that had gone wrong and all that was lost.

June wasn't sure how many times they'd gone to Huntersville Glenn, but while they'd visited only every other month, it seemed like she'd spent half her childhood there. It was a testament to just how powerful the despair of that place was. It left an imprint on a little girl's mind, an emotional scar that now made June wonder how her grandparents could have ever thought taking her there was a good idea. What benefit could it have possibly brought her to see a mother she'd never known outside of that visiting room, a nearly mute woman so distant from reality she might as well have been in a coma?

Worse still, Gramma and Grandpa never explained things. How could they? Not that June dared to ask. With her mother, things had always been that way. She was a mystery best kept to shadows, a broken skeleton in the family's closet. But at least June knew who the woman was. She could put a face to the name, however grotesque and haunted. The same could not be said about her father. Nothing was said about him at all.

She'd asked her grandparents about him once. June was in preschool. All the other kids had dads. June's earliest memory was of the chalk-white look on her grandmother's face when she'd asked. Gramma had been so pale she almost looked like June's mother. June worried she'd said something bad without realizing it, but her grandparents didn't punish her. Instead, her grandfather sat her down and explained that her father had passed away before she was born. It didn't hurt her much at the time—it was difficult to mourn someone you'd never known—

but as she'd gotten older, the void of being a virtual orphan ate at her until she was completely devoured.

Living in Killen had only exasperated her emotional problems. She'd been a depressed teen, gloomy and morbid, and despite her grandparents doing everything they could to make her home a happy one, June turned to drugs, alcohol, and promiscuity at an early age, trying to escape that black pit within. Sometimes it worked, however briefly, but most of the time her efforts only pulled her in deeper until she finally tried to physically run from it, leaving Killen and all its rotten grief behind her. It wasn't until recently that she'd decided to confront that void head-on. She was old enough now to answer her own questions, and it was too late to keep the skeletons in the closet where they belonged.

The truth hurts, she thought as she trenched through the mud of the riverbank.

The river frothed at the edges. A crow cawed, but she saw no birds. The air seemed thinner here, colder, as if she were mountain climbing instead of loping down the shore. She stopped for a rest and sat down on a boulder, her elbows on her knees as she gazed into the dreary distance.

That's when she first heard the guitar.

The sound of strumming strings reverberated off the river rocks, echoing through the chasm like the fading memory of a bad dream. June looked for the musician but saw no one. The warped, drunken sound of a slide guitar sent a chill through her she could not explain, like hearing the rattling chains of a ghost. Her skin pimpled. As the guitar went into a bluesy riff, the clamor of the water against the rocks seemed to fall into rhythm with it, creating a peculiar song.

June was suddenly dazed. Though fear remained, her mind wandered, thoughts growing foggier as she stared at the river, as if she were being hypnotized by some malevolent, unseen energy.

A barking dog brought her out of the spell. "Arf! Arf!"

But even the dog sounded wrong. It was somehow distorted, and when June turned to look, she realized why.

The woman stood just above her where the woods met the bank. She could have been fifty or eighty. Her haggard, bizarre appearance made it difficult to tell. She had a tangled briar of hair, her chin sprouting a couple of thick, white whiskers. Her eyes were locked, the left one looking to the left, the right one looking to the right, like a reptile. She had a cleft lip, and a strand of drool dangled down to her chest. She wore stained sweatpants with one leg rolled up, and a faded Disneyworld t-shirt two sizes too big.

"Arf!" she shouted again.

The strange woman grinned, pointing at June, and June stepped back in reflex. The woman kept her arm extended, still pointing as she drew closer.

"Please stay where you are," June said.

The woman chortled, the drool dangling further. She took another step, still barking. "*Arf! Arf! Arf!*"

"Get away from me," June said, backing up.

Obviously, the woman was mentally impaired. Logic told June she needn't fear her, but instincts told her to steer clear. In the woman's face, June saw generations of inbreeding, of biological ruin.

The woman's noises changed. "N-n-nuh-muh." She smiled still, her crooked teeth various shades of yellow and black. "*Nuh-muh-muh!*"

June was about to run when a man's voice called out. "Daisy!"

He emerged from the woods behind the woman, an obese man in a flannel shirt buttoned-up wrong. His belly hung over his waistband and peeked out from under his shirt. He had an under-bite and a pronounced brow like a missing link. June tensed when she noticed he was carrying something. She thought it was a rifle, then realized it was only a wooden hiking stick. He leaned on it to support his bulk.

"Daisy," he called to the woman. "You git on back now, ya hear?"

Daisy clutched her hands over her heart and shuffled over to the large man. Though he appeared younger than her, she clung to him like a child, both hands going around one of his beefy arms.

The man looked to June with jaundiced eyes. "Don't let ol' Daisy spook ya. She's a halfwit but ain't no more trouble than a ladybug."

June said nothing. It was as if she'd forgotten how to speak.

"Don't know you," the man said. "Thought I done knowed errybody on this river, but I don't know you none."

"I, um…I'm just visiting."

The man lowered his unibrow. "What's that now?"

June huffed. She'd had enough small talk. "I really must be going."

But to continue down the path, she had to pass by these hicks. She figured she could outrun them if it came to it, with the man being overweight and the woman impaired.

She tried again. "Excuse me."

The big man didn't budge, as if he hadn't heard her. "Ya ought be careful. Folks don't take kindly to visitors 'round here. Ain't errybody nice like Daisy and me." He pointed uphill. "We lives up yonder. Don't let Uncle Macon catch ya near the house now. He won't like it none."

"I'll be careful, now if you'll excuse me, please."

"Mah name's Timmy."

June started walking around him. "I don't care what your name is."

He stared at her, his eyes revealing a lack of understanding. June maneuvered around the hillbillies, her boots entering the brackish water. She moved quickly, eager to put these two behind her, and they watched as she ascended the hill, following the path to God knows where. The guitar sounds had ceased— a small relief. June heard dead leaves crackling behind her, and when she looked back, the hillbillies were following her.

Seeing June look, Daisy pointed at her again. "Arf! *Arf!*"

June moved faster so the duo couldn't keep up. Once she was out of their sight, she deviated from the trail and entered the thicket, using the trees for cover but sticking close to the river so not to lose her way. Confident she'd lost the hillbillies, she pushed her way into a clearing, then froze. Someone had stacked the area with junk. Rusted sheet metal lay amongst rotted planks of wood. A dented washer and a tube TV with a busted screen. Bald tires. Milk crates stuffed with machine parts. There were tumbleweeds of chicken wire and empty cans, with liquor bottles and hubcaps floating in puddles of mud. Half of an old, burnt-out car rested on boulders. It was a wonder how any of it had even gotten here. June guessed there must be a dirt road somewhere in these woods. She wished she knew where. It could have saved her some time.

When she saw the cabin, she got low and hid behind a stove with no door. June squinted. The same sort of garbage surrounded the cabin ahead—a hoarder's utopia. An ancient woman sat upon a moldy, flower-patterned sofa on the porch. Her body was nearly as big as Timmy's. A Pitbull with a head like a Thanksgiving turkey sat beside her.

Jesus, June thought, *even the pets are inbred.*

In the distance, Daisy barked, and the dog barked back, calling her home.

How do people live like this?

But in a way, they didn't even seem like people. To June, these backwoods freaks were subhuman at best, a genetic nightmare hidden deep in the mountains of Killen. She thought of what Timmy had said about their uncle not appreciating strangers. If Uncle Macon spotted June, would he shoot her? Rape her? *Eat* her?

She slunk back into the woods from which she came, moving in a slow crouch, and made a wide arch around the property, hoping the dog wouldn't pick up on her presence. Her hands shook as she pushed branches aside, and she breathed as softly as she could when she couldn't hold it in any longer.

There was a rumble in the distance—*thunder or a guitar?*

When June was far enough away from the cabin, she ran just as hard and fast as she'd run away from the people of Killen the first time. Only now, she was trekking deeper into this town's cold, black belly, ready to wade through the bile of the Hollow River if that's what it took.

FOURTEEN

PEACE.

That's all a man really wants, ain't it? The peace 'n quiet of the woods—my woods, his *woods. They say the wilderness is the kingdom of God. That's what I done heard as a boy. Come Sundays, the family'd all gather in the valley low and stand on the riverbank, listenin' to that crazy buzzard Deacon Jones hoot and holler 'bout the Lord. He was the first and last man I ever done feared... aside from Daddy, of course. To prove his faith in God, Jones would drink strychnine and let snakes bite him. And when he baptized you in that river, he kept you down there long 'nough to make you think you was 'bout to meet the Lord yourself.*

When it came time for me to get dunked, ol' Deacon was quotin' Corinthians. I can still hear his every word: "Be ye not unequally yoked together with unbelievers. For what fellowship has righteousness with wickedness? What common has light with darkness?"

I knew he was usin' them words to talk 'bout me. That preacher knew I was darkness even 'fore I did. So maybe he weren't all that crazy after all.

I ran away 'fore he could put me under. I was too afraid he'd drown me, and my body would stay in that cold, black river forever. Not long after that day, Deacon Jones done drown his own little ones. Killed 'em up but good. By accident or not, nobody knows. Nobody but the Deacon. Made him even crazier, I reckon. I like to think those wee babies was an offerin', like when God told Abraham to kill his son. Only Deacon done went

65

through with it, and it weren't a sacrifice to God, but a sacrifice to The River Man.

I know you know, Lori. You learned what's called for. Can't go empty-handed to that shack on the cliff now, can ya? I knew you'd make me proud and prove your love. A woman's gotta be devoted to 'er man, and I couldn't have asked for a more devoted darlin' than you.

That's why you're comin' back with me—comin' home.

***

Edmund reached his shack just as the drizzle turned to rain. The sight of the small, weathered building was enough to put a lump in his throat, the memories hitting him in warm waves—a bloody young woman screaming on the floor; dainty feet being sawed off at the ankles; a gutted body rolling down steps. Some were girls from town, others fresh faces, including a hiker who'd been foolish enough to be in these woods alone. No matter their origins, Edmund treated his darlings to the same delectable torture, testing their pain thresholds and then hammering, stabbing, and chopping beyond them. He hunted the ones with the darkest hair, Asians being his favorite, but when he desperately needed a taste, any young woman would suffice.

Edmund stepped into the fetid dank. "Home."

The smell of rot invaded his nostrils, stirring his loins and making him salivate. A red daydream fluttered through his mind, synapses crackling like lightning, and Edmund curled his hands, feeling any imaginary throat between them. New victims to decorate his shack. His heart swelled when he imagined Lori coming here, dragging along her simpleminded sister in search of a key.

Edmund had returned here with a similar goal.

Flies swarmed about the cellar door. As a child, he'd imagined it was a trapdoor like in a medieval castle, one that dropped unsuspecting victims into a torture chamber. Back then, he'd used cheese and glue traps to capture mice. Stuck in place, the rodents made for perfect practice, Edmund using sowing needles, matches, and skinning tools on them while they were still alive. As an adult, he'd moved on to human beings, but still used the same tools and methods. He was a man of tradition and appreciated the classics.

Opening the cellar door, the wretched stink of death rose about Edmund with a plume of buzzing insects. They tickled his skin. He smacked his lips as a few entered his mouth, then descended the stairs slowly, cautious of the wood rot. The rock walls of the sepulcher brought back more memories of his younger self pretending he was a cave dweller, a primitive humanoid predating homo sapiens—a *beast*. Had he reached such aspirations as an adult? The thought amused him as he landed on the cellar floor and spotted his darling.

"There you are," he said.

When he'd last seen her, she was only in a state of autolysis, the first stage of decomposition. Her muscles had stiffened with rigor mortis, but she hadn't bloated before he'd left. The frigid temperature of this underground crypt had preserved her much longer than normal, but active decay couldn't be held off forever. Now, her flesh and organs had liquified into a black pudding. Some muscle tissue remained, but the body was gray and skeletal, her tissue eaten away. Maggots swirled in the chasm of her chest. Insects and worms feasted in her sinew with gluttonous frenzy.

"Hey, baby girl," he said. "Good to see ya again."

Kneeling beside her, Edmund noticed his darling's fingernails had fallen out along with the teeth that had remained after he'd finished with her mouth. He hadn't expected that. Death was a mysterious mistress, always full of surprises. One by one, he collected the fingernails. Two dangled from the withered fingers, so he peeled them from the desiccated flesh. He drew the wad of paper from his pocket and took out his contraption of human remains—Lori's finger, Niko's teeth, Shawna's lip, and now, the fingernails of Jessica Hong.

Edmund wedged the nails into the underside of the rod of flesh and bone, piercing Shawna's lip so that the fingernails stuck out in rows like the teeth of a key.

FIFTEEN

"YOU SURE THIS IS THE RIGHT WAY?" Gary asked, riding shotgun. "I thought I saw a trail back there."

"That's the sucker way," Keith said. "Remember, I've been out here before, back when I was first hunting the bastard. The department learned about a dirt road that cuts through the woods here. Save us some time."

Gary smirked. "We don't even know where we're headed."

"There's nothing on that trail for a mile or so. Just trees and the river and a lot of rocks. This road is used by the folks who live out here. It'll get us closer to their shacks."

"And that's a good thing? These hicks don't even like it when you come asking questions in their bars and diners. We go knockin' at their homes and we're likely to get our heads blown off."

"Hey," Keith said as he turned down the dirt road, "we're not gonna get anywhere by wandering around aimlessly in these goddamned woods. We need answers, and the only way we'll get any is by talking to the locals. Some of these hicks the department interviewed before, back when we were looking for Edmund's shack. They might even remember me."

"His shack? You know where Cox lives? Or used to?"

Keith shook his head. "We never were able to find it, even

though we were out here for weeks. After a while, it seemed like we were just going in circles. These woods... they're, like... shit, I don't know how to explain it."

"What?" Gary asked, his interest stirred.

"When we were out there, we all kept getting disorientated, and the further we traveled upriver, the worse it got. It's easy to get lost out there. The sun never shines. It's some spooky shit."

Gary stared at the cop. "What're you saying?"

"Look," Keith said with a sigh. "I'm not saying these woods are haunted or cursed, but a lot of other guys believed so. And I'm not talking about some new-age hippie types or nutjob ghost hunters; I'm talking about professional men and women—homicide detectives and FBI agents and the like."

The rain picked up, its clean smell taking Gary back to a better time when he'd taken Lacy by the hips and spun her in the air. While picnicking at the park, they'd been caught in a sudden shower, and when she'd started laughing instead of getting aggravated, Gary knew he'd made the right decision. Her sundress had stuck to her, forming to her body, her long hair curling from the moisture. They were both so young then. Young and happy. After spinning her in the rain, they'd shared a long kiss, creating a memory Gary would always hold on to, for better or worse.

He forced himself back to the present. "And what about you, Keith? What do you believe?"

Keith drew a cigarette from the pack on the dashboard. "I don't know what I believe."

The dirt road wound through the desolate woodland, climbing into the hill country where the air grew colder and thinner. The terrain became increasingly difficult for a sedan until only trucks or ATVs could make it through. Keith parked, and they exited the car. Gary looked around. The trees seemed to rake the sky, their knots making hollowed-out eyes, their contorted roots like the veins of the earth.

"Nice place," Gary said, shaking his head.

"It's the unwashed asshole of the south."

Gary snickered. Maybe the cop was alright after all. Having dealt with police officers as often as he had, Gary was always leery of them. As an investigator, he'd experienced intimidation and a lack of cooperation from the law, so his distrust was not political but forged from personal experience. Cops didn't like it when a private dick meddled in their investigation. When Keith Drakeson had come knocking, Gary had expected the cop to tell him to back off the case. The offer to work together was a shock. It made him wonder what Keith was up to. Whatever it was, Gary doubted he was sticking to protocol. But Gary had never been one for rules and regulations either. Keith could prove useful. Gary would try to like him, but trust would be hard-earned.

They headed down the slope. Gary lifted the collar of his coat and tucked his hands in his pockets. The rain was sporadic but gentle. The sound of the river grew louder. When they reached the trail at the bottom of the basin, Keith pointed out a wooden sign written with paint.

Gary read it aloud. "*Into the hollow.*"

"The poetry of country bumpkins," Keith said. "It's like outsider art."

"Who do you think wrote that? Cox?"

Keith shrugged. "Who the fuck knows? All these yokels talk weird. It's like Killen has its own dialect that only gets thicker the further upriver you go."

Gary stared at the letters. They looked as if someone had fingerpainted them on.

"This shit already gives me the creeps," he said.

"Well, tighten your belt, Chatmon. It gets a whole lot worse."

Gary didn't doubt it. He was entering the homeland of a serial killer. Even aside from Cox's crimes, people had died horrible deaths here. Women had gone missing, some only teens. How many were in shallow graves that would never be found? How many were at the bottom of the river? One didn't have to believe in ghosts to be uneasy in a place with such a history of violence and grief. It was why people went silent at the memorials at Auschwitz and the World Trade Center. After he and Lacy had married, they'd found a beautiful house they could afford. The catch was the previous owner had shot his wife and three children to death inside its walls. It'd been on the market for over a year and stayed there after Gary and his wife turned it down. Standing in the woods of Killen, Gary got the same guttural feeling of dread he'd had inside that murder house.

This is a bad place, he thought. *Be careful.*

The men continued down the path in silence, listening for anything they might need to worry about—angry locals, black bears, wild boar. As always, Gary's revolver was strapped to his ankle. Though he hadn't seen Keith's piece, he was sure the cop had one on him, and still hadn't decided if that made him feel safer.

"Are we heading toward any cabins in particular?" Gary asked.

"Not exactly."

They walked side by side, sticking to the trail. It wound downward toward the river. Gary wondered if that's where the foul smell was coming from.

"So, what's the plan?" Gary asked.

"Guess we'll just have to see what happ—"

Keith froze. Gary followed the cop's gaze. His hairs stood on end when he saw the body near the riverbank. It was half-hidden behind the tree it was propped up against, but the bare, bloody legs assured him the woman was dead.

The men drew their firearms.

Keith scanned the area. "He might still be here."

Cold sweat formed at the small of Gary's back. They rounded the tree, and the more Gary saw of the corpse the more his stomach churned. He'd seen a few dead bodies in his time, but mostly in hospitals and open-casket funerals. This was a murder victim whose blood was still tacky.

But for her socks, the dead woman was stripped nude. She'd been stabbed so many times that much of her body was pulped, with one breast was removed and her genitals mutilated. Her face was in ruin, her lower lip ripped away.

"*Jesus-fucking-Christ!*" Gary said.

He retched but produced nothing. Though Keith was a veteran of homicide investigations, even he paled. They stood there helpless, dazed by the afterglow of a madman's violence.

"He's been here alright," Keith said. "This is his work."

Gary leaned on a tree as the world seemed to spin. "We need to go back. Call the feds and get a SWAT team out here."

"No."

"*No*? What do you mean *no*?"

"We're not calling this in. Not yet."

Gary blinked. "Are you nuts? Why not?"

"It'll take too long for them to get out here. Cox will be long gone by then. We're on his tail now. I don't want to lose him."

"For Christ's sake, man, *look* at this poor girl. If he's willing to do this to an innocent person, what do you think he'll do to two guys chasing him?"

"And what do *you* think he'll do to any other women he comes across, huh? If we don't go after Cox immediately, it could cost another innocent person their life. Can you live with that?"

Gary exhaled. He hated to admit it, but Keith had a point. What if they really could save a life today? Gary was painfully familiar with losing someone. He would prefer to spare other people from the same grief if he could. But he also hadn't signed up for this, had he? He hadn't expected to get this close to a serial killer. Frankly, it frightened him, as it would any sane person.

"What kind of man could do something like this?" Gary asked.

Keith's face was grim. "Calling Cox a man gives him too much credit. It humanizes him. Don't have any illusions, Chatmon. This isn't a normal human being we're dealing with. He's as close to a monster as the real world can throw at you."

"That's exactly why I don't want to go after him."

"Look, there's two of us and we've got pistols. I can't make you go, but I'm going after him."

Gary gestured toward the corpse. "We can't just leave her here."

"We also can't mess with a crime scene." Keith rolled his shoulders as if preparing his body for a fight. He pointed out the scattered items and open backpack by the dead woman. "Look at this gear. She must've been from out of town." He pointed to the shore. "There's a kayak. I'd say you could use it to paddle back to town, but it's evidence. You've got a long walk back. I suggest you get to it."

"Wait a sec—"

"Damn it, Chatmon. You knew what you were getting into when we teamed up."

"But I didn't think we'd actually find Cox here. I thought we'd find clues, not *dead bodies*."

"Things change," Keith said, turning to go.

Following him, Gary spotted something on the shore. "Oh, Jesus."

He pointed it out to Keith, and they looked down at a young, male corpse covered in blood, the belly torn open to release its contents. The stench was as bad as the sight.

"Why does he rip them to pieces like this?" Gary asked.

"Why does he kill them to begin with?" Keith said, grimacing. "*He's insane* is why. That girl back there... if we tested her eye sockets, we'd probably find Cox's semen. I keep telling you, Gary—this is a mad dog and I'm gonna put him down. Now are you coming or not?"

***

Lacy placed Gary's hand on her round belly. His wife's eyes gleamed; blue and bright and alive with excitement.

"You feel that?" Lacy asked.

Something pounded within her. *A foot.* Until that moment, her pregnancy had been more of a concept, an idea. Gary had been excited about it too, but even as Lacy had swelled up, the pregnancy seemed like an abstract daydream they'd been sharing. Now, feeling his child move for the first time, Gary was overwhelmed to the point of tears.

"Holy shit!" he said.

Lacy laughed. They both did. Gary's love for his wife, which he'd thought reached its peak on their wedding day, instantly grew even stronger. The years before Lacy hadn't been kind to him. His parents had stayed in a bad marriage all through his childhood, leaving a poor impression that had sabotaged Gary's early relationships with women. He had changed girlfriends and jobs every couple of years and moved around a lot. Drinking alone too often, sleeping in late whenever he could, avoiding family and friends, and not even checking his messages. He'd been desperately unhappy without really realizing he was clinically depressed.

Lacy had changed all of that. He now had a loving wife who'd reinvented his idea of what a romantic partnership could be. For the first time in his life, he had what could be called a happy relationship. No drama, no mind games, no power struggles. Just two people who cherished each other.

And now, that love would be shared as a family.

"Okay," Gary said. "I think it's time for you to stop working. I want you to stay home and take care of yourself, at least until I get home from work and can pamper you myself."

Lacy smiled. "Honey, you know I can't do that yet. I only get so much maternity leave."

It wasn't the first time Gary had suggested it. Lately, Lacy was coming home from her teaching job at Northeast Middle School with swollen feet and sharp back pain. He doted on her to the point where she playfully swatted him away, but Gary still didn't feel like he was doing enough in this pregnancy, despite Lacy assuring him he was a superb partner.

"Well," he said, "can't you do online classes or grade papers from home?"

Lacy gave him a smirk, which was all that was needed to remind him of how ridiculous his question was.

It was Gary's first year working at an insurance agency where he investigated fraud cases. Lacy had supported him while he was pursuing his private detective's license. He wanted to return the favor while she was building them a baby. It pained him that his salary—the largest one he'd ever had—just wasn't enough to keep them living comfortably. Lacy was right. They needed her schoolteacher income to stay afloat. But that didn't mean he had to like it.

"You know," he said, "in Bulgaria women get fifty-eight weeks of maternity leave. England has thirty-nine. But here in the good ol' U.S. of A, you only get twelve."

"Believe me," Lacy said, "I'm no happier about it than you are."

The baby kicked again, and the couple's smiles returned.

"It's going to be okay," Lacy said, kissing her husband on the cheek.

But it wasn't.

SIXTEEN

IT DIDN'T MATTER THAT HE was off duty or that the only backup he had was a middle-aged private dick with no experience in a manhunt. Keith was going to find Edmund Cox and bring him in, dead or alive. His ego demanded it. Preventing gruesome murders was fine and good, but his motivation wasn't to help others as much as it was to help himself. If he could capture Cox a second time—especially without a task force to assist him—he'd be the most famous detective in the department, maybe even the country, at least until the buzz settled down. That clout would carry a long way. He hoped it would be more than enough to get him back on duty and bury the department's investigation into the shooting of Josh Negus.

As he trekked through the hill country, Keith's thoughts wandered back to Negus even though he wanted to concentrate on Cox. The gory wreckage of the young couple by the shore had caused the memory of Negus' head spraying blood to rise out of the murk of Keith's mind.

He'd warned the son of a bitch. Long before he'd shot Negus, Keith made it very clear he wasn't to be trifled with. The flesh peddler got what was coming to him—*a bullet to the fucking head.* The little girl was an unfortunate causality, but there'd been nothing else Keith could do. Perhaps if he kept telling himself that, he might one day believe it. There'd been so many stories he'd told over the years. Some he was no longer certain were true.

Does it even matter anymore? In the end, a man becomes what he pretends to be.

Keith knew what his mission was, but what was Edmund Cox's? What deranged quest was the demon on now? Were there more obsessed groupies like Lori and Niko waiting for him out here in the sticks? Keith wondered if Cox had fucked those two before, during, or after he'd slaughtered them. It seemed unfair that this maniac had women dropping to their knees before him while Keith had to pay for sex. He wasn't a bad-looking guy. He could get girls, but the ones that gravitated to him just weren't his type. Perhaps a bit of fame would change all of that.

The rain ended, leaving Keith and Gary soggy and chilled, but still they pressed on, trying to follow a trail that was growing thin. They'd chose the way randomly after reaching a fork in the path. It was hard for Keith to tell if he'd been to this exact spot before while hunting Cox with the feds. He'd not exaggerated when he'd told Gary the woods of Killen were discombobulating. He'd seen his fellow officers lulled into a morose trance by the mere sound of that river. Keith had felt it himself too. Now his thoughts were equally muddied.

He'd just seen a young woman who'd been ripped apart. Why was he thinking about sex right now? How did Ava, the last woman he'd fucked, worm her way into his brain? Why did memories of thrusting between her thighs merge with sudden flashes of Josh Negus screaming and that little girl's head bursting open?

Olive, he thought. *Her name was Olive.*

Keith didn't want to remember her name, but with all the photos he had of the girl, he'd never forget her face.

Gary stopped walking. Keith looked back at him. Gary's face was turned toward a sky the color of concrete, and the gray light made him look even older. There was something about the lines in Gary's face that told Keith more about the man, little glimpses into a dreary inner world. They were not merely the wrinkles of time, but of heartbreak and struggle. Clearly, there was a darkness buried within the vessel of Gary Chatmon.

"What is it?" Keith asked.

Gary's eyes grew wet, his mouth hanging open.

"Chatmon?" Keith asked. "You alright?"

Gary shushed him. "Listen."

They stood in silence. Then Keith heard it—a high, fluttery voice. Someone was coming down the trail.

The voice sang, "*Oh, bury me beneath the willow, under the weepin' willow tree. So she may know where I am sleepin', and, perhaps, she'll weep for me.*"

"Cox?" Gary asked Keith.

Keith shook his head. "Doesn't sound like him."

But they clutched their pistols tight, their arms flexed, ready to strike. The singer continued.

"*Tomorrow was our weddin' day, but oh Lord, where can she be? She's gone to see that man upriver, and no longer cares for me.*"

The figure appeared on the bluff like a poltergeist. The voice had obscured their gender, but now Keith could see it was an old man. A black suit and ruffled tuxedo shirt blanketed his emaciated body, both of which were worn and dusty. The brim of his hat cast his face in shadow. Though the old man must have seen them now, he continued singing as if alone.

"*My heart is sad, and I'm in sorrow, for the only one I love. When will I see 'er? Oh, no, never. Till we meet in Heaven above.*" His song finished, the old man clapped his hands together and rubbed them as if starting a fire. "Now what all do we have here? Couple a good ol' boys out for a stroll?"

Gary spoke first. "We're just passing thro—"

Keith cut him off and addressed the stranger. "And just what is *your* business?"

"My business is not of earthly matters," the old man said. "My business is *faith*. The question is: *faith in what?*" He extended a freakishly long arm and pointed at Keith's pistol. "Out here huntin', are ya? Best be careful, son. The animals we got out here… they like to *hunt back*."

"I'm not your son, pops." Keith drew his billfold and flashed his badge. "I'm here on police business."

When the old man raised his chin, the shadow of his brim moved, revealing a decrepit face covered in sores and bug bites. Keith recoiled. The man offered a rotting grin.

"Another constable come down to the ol' Hollow," the old man said. "*Like a muddied spring or polluted fountain is a righteous man who gives way before the wicked.*" His horrible smile widened. "*I pursued my enemies and overtook 'em, and did not turn back 'til they were consumed.*"

Keith narrowed his eyes. "What is all that?"

"Proverbs. Psalms. My, Jesus, my—I suggest you study your bible, son. I do declare this to be a choice day for it."

"You some kind of preacher?"

"Oh, where *are* my manners?" The old man tipped his hat with a small bow. "Name's Deacon Jones. I'm a messenger 'round these parts."

"Well, I've got a message for you," Keith said. "Go home right now and lock all your doors and windows. There's a situation out here—a dangerous one."

Jones chuckled. "Every situation is a dangerous one. Whether we know it or not, the terrors of this world are always at our backs, lurkin' in all the sweet pleasures of the dark."

Keith exhaled. This was exactly the sort of crazy talk he'd come to expect of the hayseeds of Killen. "This is serious, old-timer. There's a killer out he—"

"Death don't have no mercy in this land."

These words made Keith's skin pimple. There was something familiar about the phrase, something he feared he didn't want to remember.

"What'd you say?" he asked.

Jones shook his head. "What we don't learn from the good book, we learn through song, my son. His music speaks to us. One only need listen."

The preacher moved past them, drifting like fog in a bad dream, humming along his way.

"Stick to the trail," Gary shouted after him.

"Yeah," Keith said, realizing Gary was trying to steer Jones away from the crime scene. Though Keith wouldn't have jurisdiction here even if he were on active duty, he tried to give an order. "Stay away from the riverbank, preacher man. Go home or go to town, but don't stay out in these woods."

"I've always been in these here woods, and always will be." Jones looked back at them, his eyes like gleams on a blade. "Whoever ya'll are lookin' for, don't judge 'em too harshly now. Remember the Gospel of Luke: *Those enemies of mine who did not want me to be king over them—bring them here and kill them in front of me.* Ya'll know who said that?"

"Who?"

The preacher flashed his rictus grin. "'Twas Christ himself."

Keith's stomach went hollow.

"See?" Jones asked. "Even Jesus was a killer when it suited him. And no man would stoop so low as to lay judgement upon our savior." He turned his back to them and proceeded down the path. "Ya'll got a ways to go yet. Sing a merry tune to keep on track." He returned to singing. "*Yes, we'll gather at the river. The beautiful, beautiful river…*"

Keith shouted over him but did not pursue. "Do what I said, old man! Get behind closed doors."

"*Gather with the man at the river…*"

As Jones descended the trail, he veered right at the fork Keith and Gary had barely discerned within the falling leaves. The preacher sang on as he wandered into the black embrace of the woods, his gospel tune fading until all Keith could hear was the constant, gentle roar of the river, a sound like a screaming crowd.

Gary stepped into him. "You just let him go?"

Keith continued to watch Jones as the preacher slipped between the trees. "We don't have time for him. We gotta keep moving."

"That old bastard is nuts. All that talk about death and murder. What if he's the one who butchered that poor couple back there?"

Keith huffed. "C'mon, Chatmon. That geezer couldn't swat a mosquito. Didn't you see how old and frail he was? Two young, fit people would knock his dick in the dirt."

"That may be, but he might still have something to do with it. I mean, what if he's in cahoots with Cox?"

"No chance," Keith said. "Edmund Cox does not play well with others."

"But—"

"Leave the police work to me, will ya? With all respect to private eyes, ya'll don't work a lot of murder cases these days. I'm a homicide detective—a professional. I know what I'm doing."

But Keith wasn't sure that was true; not when it came to Edmund Cox.

"And what about The River Man?" Gary asked.

Keith rolled his eyes. "The ghost story again?"

"You know as well as I do it has something to do with all of this. That preacher was singing about a man on a river."

"There must be a million gospels about rivers, Chatmon. It's a coincidence."

"He kept telling us to listen for his music. That we should sing too."

"He also told us to read our bibles. You gonna skip along to the nearest church house?"

Gary sighed. "I'm just saying this seems like more than coincidence. That preacher quoted an old blues lyric. 'Death Don't Have No Mercy' is a song by Blind Gary Davis, a bluesman who died half a century ago. I know because Jessica Hong wrote about it in her essay on hill country blues. It's about the inevitability of death and grief and suffering. And I was listening to it *just last night*. Is that a coincidence too?"

Keith grumbled, trying to hide the chill that had just coursed through him. "You're not suggesting that old man was spying on you before we came out here, are you?"

"Course not," Gary said. "In a way, that's my whole point."

"Well, it's a point I don't get." He started walking. "C'mon. We're losing light. We gotta stay focused."

"We also must acknowledge the things we're witnessing. How else will we ever understand?"

Keith continued uphill but his eyes returned to the river below.

"Maybe we don't want to understand," he said.

SEVENTEEN

IT WAS HARD TO TELL IF DUSK was coming or if the thickening rain-clouds caused the slate skies. June supposed it didn't matter. Night would fall soon either way. There was no holding back darkness. She'd learned that at an early age.

Having wandered off the trail to avoid the inbred family, June moved through the woodland with no other guide than her internal compass. All her life she'd felt it—a *pull* toward something she could not name but felt deep within like a convulsive fetus. There was a time she'd fought against this pull, believing what her grandparents always said about her independence, that she was more than the sum of her ancestry. June's wanderlust was not solely the result of growing up in a shit town full of shit people. She'd also been fighting against an inexplicable urge that took her to all those sordid places young girls weren't supposed to go. But now she was back in Killen, the last place any decent girl would be, let alone return to. That strange pull had brought her here, luring her more strongly than ever before. June wasn't forced to follow it; she wanted to. It was more than impulse; it was instinct. She'd never felt so primal, but then she'd never felt all that human to begin with.

June pressed through the thicket as the light faded from the world around her. Spotting what might have been a trail, she followed it through a curtain of naked trees. They seemed to grow larger and more misshapen the further she ventured up-river. Mossy stones gave way to black boulders that sulked within the dead forest like cemetery tombs. June peered through the wilderness, a cautious solider in a foreign land. She'd come from Killen, but this place was no home to her. Nowhere ever had been. For June, the very concept of *home* was a figment.

She crested the hill. Then she spotted a shack.

June stopped. She looked all around, half expecting another hillbilly to come barking at her. The woods were gloomy and silent, and the rustic hovel ahead seemed as peaceful as a mausoleum. She relaxed when she saw the shack's general decay. Foil on the broken windows. Door hanging wide open. Even the most backwoods hick couldn't live in a place this dilapidated. The shack leaned to one side like a suicide jumper on a ledge, as if the weight of one more fallen leaf on its roof would cause it to collapse.

It must be abandoned, right? she asked herself.

Perhaps possums had made a nest inside, but it seemed impossible that a human being could live here anymore.

What if this is the one?

The thought chilled her.

This couldn't be the place. According to June's research, the FBI had combed these woods searching for the cabin home of Edmund Cox only to turn up nothing. June had been out here just half a day.

A moan of thunder turned her eyes skyward.

"Darkness falls," she said to herself, then wondered where that had come from.

Her own thoughts confused her sometimes. Odd phrases came to her out of the ether and exited her mouth without conscious effort. June often talked herself, muttering and whispering, barely even paying attention to what she was saying. Sometimes she had trouble separating the previous night's dream from an actual memory. Oftentimes, she would enter a place with no recollection of why she'd gone there. Her mind could completely shift focus when she went from one place to the next. She would need to pee and then go to the bathroom only to wonder why she'd gone into it, and then she'd brush her teeth instead, not even realizing her error until she'd already left the bathroom and her bladder reminded her. Not even twenty years old and she already had concerns about Alzheimer's and dementia. June doubted either was the root of her problems, but she also didn't want to believe the things people had told her about her strange, wandering thoughts.

The thunder intensified, causing the tree limbs to shudder. The earth seemed to roll beneath her feet. As the rain began again, June looked to the black chasm of the shack's open doorway and took a deep breath.

She started toward it. The rotted wood had caused the structure to bow and wither. There were several abandoned hornet nests beneath the awning. Even the insects didn't want to be here anymore. June stared into that black hole of a doorway, but the darkness was impenetrable to the naked eye.

You've taken shelter in worse, she told herself.

She'd slept in dumpsters behind fast-food restaurants after feasting on the evening's fresh throwaways. A stolen tarp had been her only consistent shelter in the desert towns of Nevada and Arizona. She'd stayed six weeks under a causeway in Georgia, preferring it to an acquaintance's house where she was expected to pay her share of the rent with her body. Once, in shitass Oklahoma, she'd deigned to using a shipping container for a tent. At least this shack had once been a home. No matter how many spiders and rusty nails she might have to look out for, it was an actual building she could stay dry in, preventing her from freezing in the cruel November climate.

June took a step closer.

For whatever reason, she remained hesitant. She was annoying herself. All the hardship and madness she'd seen, and she couldn't face some shitty riverside shack?

"Because it's his," she said aloud.

It was as if someone else had said it. June hadn't thought the words first, but simply blurted them out like a belch.

It can't be Edmund's shack, she thought.

But she was having a difficult time convincing herself. Logic told her to get out of the rain, but a queer feeling had coiled about June's spine like an earthworm. It made little sense. She'd come out here hoping to find the man, so why should she be afraid of drawing closer by finding his allusive shack?

Because he might be in there.

Wanting to meet the killer was not the same as being thrown into his lap. It was much easier to want a thing than it was to do it. Reality didn't bend to the expectations of one's fantasies. That's why people always said to be careful what you wished for.

The raindrops grew heavier, their touch like ice.

June approached the doorway. Gramma would have crossed herself before entering a place like this, but June wasn't her grandmother. She clutched the loops of her backpack and stepped into a darkness rich and pure. Her eyes didn't have time to adjust. A foul stench struck her like a fist, forcing her to retreat out of the doorway. June wasn't sensitive to stink—a girl who treated a dumpster like a bed-and-breakfast couldn't afford to be—but this odor was overpowering. She heard flies buzzing. The air possessed a metallic flavor.

Turning away from the shack, June fled the stench for fear of more of it entering her lungs, worrying it could cause physical harm like toxic mold. She spat to get any residual particles out of her mouth, and when she collected herself, she simply stared at the shack's fetid vortex.

June knew that smell. There was no longer any doubt who this place belonged to.

You have to go in.

It was the last thing she wanted to do, but the most logical step if she were to continue. She'd come too far to quit. Sighing, June drew the collar of her shirt over her nose and mouth like a mask. She trembled as she returned to the doorway, listening closely, hearing only the frenetic symphony of flies. She held her breath as she stepped into the shack of Edmund Cox—the secret hideout of a serial murderer.

It was empty.

There was some decrepit furniture and discarded junk, and a

small table with black ooze where something organic had liquified. But that wasn't the source of the odor.

The stench was coming from the open cellar door—the ripe aroma of death.

June was familiar enough with this brand of stink to recognize it at the offset. Perhaps an animal had crawled down into the cellar to die, but she doubted that. Anywhere else, that would be the obvious guess, but this was no normal place. Edmund's shack was an abode of suffering and pain, a cradle of depravity so soused in death it had become a living hellscape.

She approached the open cellar, another black vortex beckoning her. Each step was the crossing of an ocean. Her mouth had gone dry, all the blood leaving her cheeks. When she reached the edge, June stared down at the rickety steps and wet walls of limestone. Here the flies were at their most crazed. The cellar was their home now, as was whatever—or *whomever*—had drawn them here.

Her toes touched the edge, but she went no further.

This is what you wanted, June reminded herself. *This is why you're here.*

It was insanity, but all her life had been. She was finally trying to make some sense of it all, and that had become more important to her than her own safety.

The truth hurts.

She put out one foot, then quickly drew it back. Instead of descending the stairs, June lowered the collar of her shirt and called into the buzzing blackness below.

"Edmund?" she asked the void.

Her voice startled the insects, and their buzzing grew louder, like television static at top volume. June had never wanted to leave a place as badly as she did right now, not even when she'd run away from home. But that inner drive persisted, refusing to let her leave. She had to know for sure.

"Edmund Cox?" she called out. "Are you down there?"

Only the flies replied. An army of them rose from the rotted depths in a black plume, engulfing June and causing her to shut her eyes. But she did not waver. She stayed at the foot of the steps, her fists clenched, heart thumping. The flies moved all about her.

"I ain't a cop," she said into the opening below. "I'm alone and unarmed."

She opened one eye, peeking into the nothingness, unsure what she expected.

"I just wanna meet you," she said.

The truth hurts.

A sudden flash of lightning spilled pink light through the cabin's open front door and uncovered windows, knifing through every slat in the cabin's beams. When it subsided, it tinted the interior of the shack red like a photographer's dark room. June blinked, thinking her eyes were playing tricks on her, but the crimson glow remained. Trembling, she looked around her for the source of the light, but its effect was omnipresent. Something trickled onto the top of her head.

Rain, she thought. But rain wasn't warm.

June looked up. More drops sprinkled her cheeks and wet her lips. A salty, coppery taste made her spit. She stepped back to avoid the leak, but when she looked around, every inch of the shack was now glistening. Red puddles pooled on the floor. Every board perspired blood, every crevice bubbling with gore.

Another lightning flash, and the rotted walls contorted, the wood twisting and snapping to create mask sculptures of screaming faces. Shadows twisted in dark, forming broken bodies and discarded human parts—an imprint of the countless horrors these walls had concealed. June had experimented with every type of drug she could get her hands on, but she'd never experienced hallucinations this vivid, and though she'd had her share of nervous breakdowns, she'd never witnessed anything this evil. The screams of dead women and the roar of the flies that had devoured them drowned out June's gasp. She cried out but couldn't be sure if it were her tears or the blood of victims that rolled down her cheeks.

Thunder rumbled, only it wasn't thunder. The strumming of a guitar echoed through the hill country like a weather siren, filling the shack with reverberations that shuddered June's heart.

The acoustic sound gave way to a crackling, electric roar, and June stumbled backward, just catching herself. She had the terrible feeling that if she fell, she could never get back up, that the sopping, red floorboards would swallow her into this nightmare realm where tortured women thrashed and sobbed and died forever.

June ran.

The redness blurred as she raced toward the subtle gray light of the doorway, and when she passed over the threshold, cold rain blasted her. The chill felt good, cleansing. It meant she was back to the normal world—or at least as normal as Killen allowed. The dead woodland was grim, but the redness had fled. Out here, there was only the gray ruin of reality.

Still, June ran on. She was tempted to look back at the cabin, to see if the crimson glow remained, but she didn't want to see it ever again, fearing that to witness it once more would invite the redness to permeate her life completely and indefinitely. And so, she continued into the deep thicket, holding her hands over her racing heart.

"Mom," she whimpered.

EIGHTEEN

EDMUND NEEDED A BOAT.

He could go back to Shawna and her boyfriend and take theirs, but he hated to backtrack. His quest was one of forward motion, constant progress. The rain was freezing, but the key grew warm in his pocket, cozying against his body like the many lovers it'd been forged from. Edmund patted it as he continued along the shore. Visiting home had been a nostalgic treat, but he had no intentions of returning there again. The shack had served its purpose. Now it could be abandoned, like the handle of a knife that had broken off inside its victim.

He thought of Lori again, his darling one weighing heavy on his mind. Edmund felt no remorse and had no regrets. He was confident Lori wouldn't have either. Thoughts of her were of the erotic variety, memories of her taut, blood-slick skin pressed against his own. Her love had been the most delectable of flavors. He would long savor its aftertaste.

The river rolled on, its murk the color of molasses. Leaves swirled in the froth, the colors they'd held in October now faded to a brown decay. All was ashen and dull. Edmund was looking forward to the shroud of crimson that awaited him in The River Man's realm. He'd seen it only once before, a red glow that permeated the boundaries of the known world, propelling the right travelers into a seductive dimension of pure horror.

Therein lied the dream and the power.

The River Man's power.

His power.

As Edmund proceeded up the bank, he hummed the songs of his youth. They were ballads of murder, romance, and God—three things he'd since learned were not mutually exclusive. These old songs told stories. Edmund liked that. Singing them reminded him of his family. For all their abuses and the wrongs they'd done him as a boy, Edmund carried their memories always, having been raised to believe in the importance of family. But it was a hell of a lot easier to love kinfolk when they were underground. Sometimes he longed for some semblance of family. The Cox bloodline had thinned down until he was the last drop. He would have liked to carry on the family name, but even the fantasy of building a family of his own was ludicrous. His only brides were the darlings he diced and pulverized, his only loved ones the chunks of human remains in his pocket. So, instead of continuing the family name, he gave it legacy. Broken bones and expunged organs forged the Cox family crest. The name would curdle blood for generations to come.

Putting a hand up to shield his eyes from the rain, Edmund saw a black shape moving upon the surface of the Hollow River. Squinting, he could just make out two people in a rowboat, one large and one small. They had on rain slickers with the hoods up, reminding Cox of Klansmen. Fishing poles dangled over the edge of the boat. It seemed they'd gone out to catch some catfish only to get caught in the storm, and now they were retreating to the shore.

Edmund slunk into the shadows of the woods, watching the duo draw near. He slid the butcher knife from his belt and smiled when he heard a familiar voice.

"Arf! Arf!"

It'd been many years since Edmund had seen Daisy Boone, but he remembered her penchant for barking. When he was young, the Boones had lived downriver, and like most people in the woods of Killen, they kept to themselves. The disgraceful clan of inbred cretins had always kept a ridiculous amount of junk and garbage around their property like a border wall of filth, warning off outsiders. Sometimes Edmund had seen Macon Boone and his fat nephew Timmy waddling through the woods, hunting frogs and possums for supper, but he'd never spoken with them. Daisy, however, was as gregarious as she was simple. She'd always waved to him and the other kids when they gathered on the riverbank to play, and she watched Deacon Jones' baptisms from afar, clapping and barking as the congregation took turns being held underwater.

Once Edmund began his killings, he avoided the Boones altogether, not wanting to be noticed by anyone, but the whole family was so genetically stunted that Edmund doubted they had the brain power to pose any threat, even if Macon was an ornery coot. Besides, people in these parts didn't call the police. Whether it was moonshine or a murder, everyone in the Killen woods had something to hide.

Edmund watched as the boat drew closer to the shore. Daisy barked and brayed.

"I'm goin', I'm goin'!" Timmy said, paddling as quickly as his bulk allowed. "I done told ya, Daisy—ya shoulda gone to the jakes 'fore we went out on the water. Ya just ain't never listen none!"

Daisy bounced in her seat, barking and pointing at the woods. Edmund chuckled at the absurdity. Here was a boat being offered to him as if he had his own fairy godmother. The river was on his side. It wanted him to succeed.

Timmy slowed as they reached the shore, the bow bouncing off the rock. Daisy sprung up quickly for such an old woman. She wadded through the water and sprinted up the slope in a crooked crab-walk, like someone running over hot coals. Timmy remained hunched-over in the boat, his head hung, face hidden behind his hood. Edmund remained hidden too, crouching behind a briar of thorns as the old woman staggered by. She removed her rain slicker and dropped her sweatpants to her ankles, then squatted and began urinating. Little pig snorts escaped her, and when Edmund glimpsed her face, he noted her lizard eyes and the strand of drool dangling from her chin.

A premonition hit him.

Perhaps the river was blessing him with yet another darling.

The woman was far from Edmund's type. She was old and beyond ugly, a genetic freak with the mind of a toddler. But wouldn't that make her even more special to the dark forces he aimed to appease? Would she not bring a more considerable reward? He evaluated her worth. In "civilized" society, a woman like Daisy Boone would be a virgin, but this was the backwoods of Killen, and Daisy came from a family that wouldn't object to fucking an actual dog, let alone a human being who acted like one. Edmund did not doubt Timmy and Macon had been inside the derelict. He only wondered if she'd enjoyed it or not.

She certainly wouldn't enjoy what Edmund could do to her.

He drew the wad of paper from his pocket, bypassing the key, and placed Lori's eye atop a slab of stone, pointing it toward Daisy.

You're with me darlin', he thought, speaking to Lori internally. *I don't want you to miss a thing.*

Edmund crept through the woods as the halfwit voided her bladder, the ammonia stink of her piss strong enough to break through the rain. The handle of the knife grew warm inside his fist. As she finished, the old woman stood, and Edmund came in behind her, reaching between her legs with his free hand and using the other to shove the tip of the blade into the back of her neck. The rain pounded, drowning her squeals, and as Edmund started on her the thunder returned, boisterous, applauding his sin.

He finished with her before Timmy even got his fat ass out of the boat.

Timmy called for Daisy from the shore, asking if she was done peeing. Clearly, he hadn't heard the noises she'd made in the last excruciating moments of her life. Edmund wiped the blood from his blade and pulled up his pants, collected Lori's eye, and then put on Daisy's rain slicker before heading downhill, a reaper drifting through the rain like black mist. He was far bulkier than Daisy Boone, but by the time Timmy realized there was someone else under that slicker, the imbecile's throat was slashed. Edmund didn't have time to rip through Timmy's considerable mass, so he ended his life quickly and held the rowboat in place as the fat man fell overboard. Timmy thrashed, so Edmund stepped on the small of his back and held his head under the lapping waves, watching as the water bloomed red like a carnation.

Climbing into the boat, Edmund stared at the choppy waters ahead, his eyes as black as the walls of rock that would grow higher and higher as he proceeded upriver. In his pocket, the flesh key burned like a hot razor, electrified by the addition of Daisy Boone's withered nipple.

He patted it like a dog's head.

"Arf, arf," he said.

NINETEEN

THE TREMOR IN HIS WIFE'S VOICE chilled Gary's flesh. Before Lacy could even explain what was happening, he heard gunshots over the phone.

"Gary," she said. "Gary…"

"Lacy," he said helplessly. "Oh my God, honey—"

His wife spoke directly, and though her voice trembled, he could tell she was trying to sound calm, for his sake and those of the children in her classroom.

"There's an active shooter in the school," she said.

Gary's heart skipped a beat. "Oh, Jesus… honey, are you hurt?"

"We're okay," she said. "The students have trained for this. We're hiding in—"

A barrage of rapid gunshots cut her off. Gary heard screams. A male voice was yelling above the chaos, but Gary couldn't tell what was being said.

"Lacy!" Gary cried.

This time when she spoke, her fear couldn't be contained. He heard his wife's tears, a sound that would haunt him to his grave.

"I love you, Gary," she said. "I don't know if—"

There was a loud burst, followed by the staccato of an assault rifle. Children screamed. A boy cried for his mother, then fell silent as a shot rang out. Lacy shouted at her students to run. The gunfire continued. Gary cried his wife's name, wanting her to say anything to let him know she was still alive. When she finally spoke, he wasn't the one she was talking to.

"Tyler," she said between gunshots. "Tyler, don't do thi—"

Another blast and Lacy screamed in pain. "No! My baby! *Please, my baby!*"

"Lacy!" Gary choked on his tears. "Oh, God, Lacy! *Lacy!*"

The last time he heard his wife's voice, she was begging for the life of their unborn child.

***

The memory often returned to Gary, choking his waking hours and infiltrating his dreams. Perhaps it was the sight of the dead bodies by the shore that had caused his wife's final moments to rise to the forefront of his thoughts, or perhaps it was the influence of the river itself.

That's what Jessica Hong's essay claimed. The realm of The River Man was said to drag the darkest memories from the depths of one's soul, no matter how thoroughly you'd buried them. Was that why he kept thinking he heard his wife whisper to him from behind the treeline? They were short, one-word breaths, like the sweet nothings she'd once said to him in bed, before fourteen-year-old Tyler Wilson brought his father's AR-15 to class, taking the lives of seventeen students, four teachers, and one fetus. But each time Gary turned his head toward the sound of his late wife's voice, it would transform into a whistle of wind, nothing more.

What was he doing out here, trekking through freezing rain, a partner to some renegade cop with a death wish? He should be on his way to the nearest police station to report the double homicide they'd stumbled upon, not wandering in the woods. He'd thought he could find something that would give the Hong family closure. Maybe he'd just wanted to offer some semblance of peace to another family, having suffered a tragedy of his own.

Whatever his motivation had been, it was now clear to Gary that all he was doing here was putting himself in danger. Even without the threat of Edmund Cox, there was a veil of evil to this forest he could no longer deny, despite it going against everything he believed in. Everywhere he looked, destruction and atrocity lingered like a coat of grease. Killen's heritage was malevolence, its history awash in blood and poison.

"I think it's high time we turned back," he said.

Keith stopped. "We've been over this already."

"Well, I don't think it's up for debate anymore. If you want to pursue this maniac, that's your business, but—"

"But you're a coward."

Gary narrowed his eyes at the insult. "You don't know me."

"But I know your kind." A darkness moved across Keith's face. "Too old and afraid to take risks."

"*Risks?* For Christ's sake, man, we're not gambling with poker chips—we're risking *our lives* out here. All we've found are two dead bodies and a crazy old preacher. Whatever trail Cox left, we've lost it, and now it's getting dark."

"I haven't lost jack shit," Keith said, pointing at Gary. "I don't lose, Chatmon. I *never* lose."

Gary's brow furrowed, his growing dislike for Keith Drakeson now saddled with concern for the young man's mental state. He was beginning to feel unsafe around him. Though Keith had made no direct threats, his demeanor suggested a capacity for violence.

"Fine," Gary said. "You're the cop. You hunt this madman."

"So that's just it for the Hong family, huh? You're just gonna give up on them?"

"I'm not arguing this with you anymore, and I'm not gonna freeze to death in these wet clothes by staying out here all night."

Keith snickered. "You ain't goin' no place."

The hairs on Gary's neck stood up. He stared at Keith, his eyes like slits.

"What're you gonna do, huh?" Keith asked. "You gonna walk back alone? In the dark? With Edmund Cox still out there? Even if you avoid him, what do you think your chances are of getting lost out here? And how many miles do you think it is back to town, huh? Ten? Fifteen?"

Though Keith made a good argument, Gary wasn't about to give him the satisfaction.

"I'm going back," he said.

Turning around on the trail, Gary kept one eye on the cop. The small amount of trust between them had crumbled. He expected Keith to persist, maybe even give him a police order to continue through these godforsaken woods. Instead, there was only silence between them, but this time when Gary heard a woman's voice, Keith heard it too, and they turned toward the sound just as a young woman emerged from the brush.

She was pale with midnight hair, her eyes wide. Gary figured her to be twenty at the most. Clad in all black, the wet clothes hung on her small body like potato sacks. When she saw the two men, she gasped and stumbled backward, falling on her butt. The men came toward her.

"You alright?" Gary asked.

Her wide eyes bounced from Gary to Keith and back again.

"It's okay," Keith assured her. "I'm a cop."

When he extended a hand to help her up, she flinched and moved out of his reach.

"Don't fuckin' touch me," she snapped.

"Take it easy," Keith told her. "We're just trying to help you."

"Yeah, right." She got to her feet on her own. "I don't want your help."

"Look, I can show you my badge if you think I'm lying about being a cop."

"Don't make no difference to me if you are or not."

She looked at the pistols the men were carrying, and Gary felt suddenly ashamed of his, but not enough to holster it.

"You shouldn't be out here," Keith told her.

She sneered. "It's a free country."

"You don't seem like you live around here."

"Neither do you."

She hitched her backpack higher and continued along the

trail, following the river. Gary and Keith looked at each other, shrugged, and followed her.

"Please," Gary said to the young woman, "just listen to us for a second."

She picked up her pace. Gary knew she could outrun them if she wanted to, but having seen their guns, she was probably too afraid to do so.

"There's a maniac on the loose," Gary said. "You're not safe out here."

She kept walking but looked back at him the same way Gary had looked back at Keith when he'd decided to go.

"Two bodies!" Keith called out to her. "Two bodies downriver. One was a woman close to your age. He ripped her guts out. Tore her face up. Took one of her tits off."

Gary grimaced. He didn't know if this shock tactic was having the desired effect. It might just make the girl even more afraid of them.

"He's not lying," Gary told her. "Please, you don't know what's out here."

She stopped and turned to face him. "I know *exactly* what's out here."

The men looked at her quizzically. Her eyes were the temperature of Nordic ice, reflecting the dying light of day. She was a pretty girl. Gary hated to think what Edmund Cox would do to her.

"Just what do you think that is?" Keith asked her.

She narrowed her eyes at him. "Ain't a soul in Killen don't know 'bout Edmund Cox. And don't bother tellin' me he escaped neither. I know it. Don't need you or nobody to explain nothin' to me, ya hear?"

Gary and Keith shared another concerned glance.

"Who are you?" Keith asked. "What's your name?"

"My *name*? *Fuck You*, that's my name."

Keith glowered. "You're old enough to know better than to mouth off to an officer."

"I ain't gotta give ya my name if I ain't done nothin'. That's the law. I know my fuckin' rights."

Though the girl's tone was assertive, she was trembling. Sensing a mean heat rising in Keith, Gary intervened before the girl could instigate him any further. He felt like a parent getting between feuding children, feeling his age around these younger people. Did seniority put more pressure on him to do what was right?

"Just calm down, okay?" he said to the girl. "He's a cop but I'm not, and nobody is trying to hassle you here. My name's Gary. This is Kei—"

"Detective Keith Drakeson," Keith corrected.

Gary continued. "He's not exaggerating when it comes to those two murder victims. Please, you'll be much safer with us."

Though he wanted to get out of these woods, the girl's arrival had shifted his priorities. He couldn't leave her out here with Cox wandering around. The threat of another woman suffering at the killer's hand was no longer a hypothetical. The girl even fit Cox's type—not Asian, but young and skinny with black hair. Unless she came with them, the odds favored her dying out here.

"I ain't goin' nowhere with you," she said. "How do I know you ain't a couple of perverts? I don't know you from Adam."

"But you *do know* Edmund Cox, so you know what he'll do to you if he finds you out here alone."

Keith nodded. "He'll show you what a real pervert is. Then he'll kill you."

Again, Gary wished the cop would ditch the tough-as-nails routine. Reasoning with the girl seemed a better course of action.

"If he kills me," she said, "then that's my problem."

Gary shook his head. "You're wrong. It's our problem too. I couldn't live with myself if I left you out here and you ended up dead too."

And it was true. He wasn't just trying to find closure for the family who'd hired him; now he was also trying to save others from the violence of a madman. He almost told the girl the complete story then—Lacy being killed, their baby dying, his troubles with drugs and alcohol, the unending grief that stayed with him like a disease.

Gary never shared this information with people, so the sudden urge to surprised him. As if sensing this, the girl's face softened, the flare leaving her nostrils. She crossed her arms and looked the men up and down.

She sighed. "I'm headed upriver."

Keith spoke before Gary could. "Perfect. That's where we're going too."

TWENTY

HER NAME WAS JUNE. That was the only information she was willing to give Keith regarding her identity. She looked fresh out of high school and yet weathered somehow, like she'd graduated in handcuffs. Keith knew a runaway when he saw one. Worn backpack, messy hair, black clothes, a hint of body odor. June may as well have had "halfway house" stamped on her forehead. He'd seen countless other girls just like her. They were never in short supply.

"So, what're you doing out here anyway?" he asked, though he had an idea what her answer might be.

June looked him in the eyes, which Keith respected. She had a face like Billie Eilish—attractive yet somehow bitchy, like those magazine models that never smiled. It was the kind of face Keith would like to slap, though not out of anger. Not yet.

"That's my business," she said.

They were walking along the trail again. Gary Chatmon's whining about turning back was on a temporary hold now that June had arrived. The private dick seemed to have delusions about what it meant to be a good man. He could leave Keith out here alone, but not the girl.

"I think I know exactly why you're out here," Keith explained to her.

The river grew louder as they descended toward the shoreline, a natural static that echoed like the remnants of a bad dream.

"You keep thinkin' that," June said.

She had the same snooty air about her that all halfway decent-looking females of her generation did. It was as if they fed off rejecting men even when they weren't being hit on. Was it sheer arrogance or an elaborate cock tease? Either way, it boiled Keith's blood, making him want to smack her pretty, little face even more.

"You're a groupie, ain't ya?" he asked, more statement than question.

She huffed.

Typical young cunt, Keith thought.

"I'm right, aren't I?" he asked.

June just kept walking. "Whatever."

"No. Not *'whatever'*. You're one of these serial killer groupies. Obsessed with true crime cases, am I right? Listen to all your podcasts. Tally up your favorite murderers like you're collecting baseball cards."

Gary tried to interject. "Keith…"

"What?" Keith shrugged. "She's not denying it."

June smirked, refusing to look at him, but she rubbed her neck, a sure sign of irritation. A twitchy feeling overcame Keith's extremities.

"Would you like to know what Edmund Cox does with his groupies?" he asked her.

June spun to face Keith. "*He fucks them and dismembers them.* Is that what you're gonna say? I told you I know who he is—*what* he is."

"I'll bet you do. Let's see what's in that backpack."

"Go fuck yourself."

Keith snickered. Again, Gary tried to make peace, but Keith ignored him. So did June.

"You've no cause to search me," she said.

"Your lawyer ain't out here, honey," Keith told her. "I'm looking for a killer and I need to know you're not working with him. Now open that bag."

"I said, go *fuck* yourself!"

She hurried on but Keith stepped in front of her. "Listen up, little girl. Whatever rules and regulations you think you know so well—they don't apply out here. Not under these conditions. Now I ain't asking, I'm *telling* you—give me the fuckin' bag, *now.*"

If he had to put an exclamation point on things, he could get rough with her, but he was hoping it wouldn't come to that, especially with Gary as a witness. June stared at Keith, the hatred in her eyes like an aphrodisiac. If he couldn't get young women to like him, he would settle for their hatred. At least it kept them thinking about him. And though Gary was far more patient, he didn't object to Keith's request. It seemed he understood the reasoning behind a search.

June didn't offer the backpack, but when Keith reached for it, she didn't fight him. He gently pulled it down her shoulder blades, and her arms went behind her, reminding him of all the times he'd put other pretty things like her in handcuffs. It was amazing what teenage girls would do to keep from having to call their parents from jail.

Keith put the backpack on the ground and unzipped it. "Anything in here that could poke or stab me? Any needles or anything like that?"

June's only answer was that slack, dead face of hers. Keith didn't let that deter him, and when he drew the folder and envelopes out of the backpack, the magazine and newspaper clippings within were no surprise. He held them up so Gary could see.

"What'd I tell ya?" Keith said. "Another goddamned groupie."

Gary shook his head like a disappointed father. June remained cold. She showed no shame. No emotion at all.

"You done?" she asked Keith.

He sifted through the rest of the bag—a half-empty bottle of water; a baggie of cashews; an old rag; mini bottles of body wash from a motel; a toothbrush; some tampons. A true hobo satchel.

She had no hiking supplies at all. No compass or flashlight or flints. Keith doubted the girl even had a phone.

But she had plenty of information about Edmund Cox.

Just what the world needs—another Manson family bitch.

Cox had snagged another slut to give him head before he took hers off. The insanity of it repulsed Keith. He wondered what he might have done to June if Gary wasn't there too, how he might have disciplined her for her wicked ways. One thing Keith knew about women was that some of them needed punishment to learn anything. What form the punishment took depended on how attractive they were. This girl was not just Edmund Cox's type, but also Keith's. He liked them young. He also liked them to be wrong just so he could set them right again. Bad girls needed powerful men to turn them into good women. Despite all the liberated nonsense they regurgitated when other sisters were listening, behind closed doors, *every* female wanted to be dominated and corrected by a man. In Keith's experience, the young ones didn't always realize that was what they needed. He figured that was why he struggled with dating, but also thought it made him a better cop.

Satisfied, Keith closed the bag and handed it back to June, and she snatched it from him like a squirrel about to run off with an acorn.

"Gotta frisk ya," Keith said.

Her face reddened. "No *fuckin'* way. Forget it."

"How do I know you don't have a weapon?"

"Hey, you guys have guns."

"Never mind that. We're talking about you. I just need to give you a quick pat down."

Frisking girls like her was one of the perks of the job. He'd copped plenty of feels as a beat cop. Sometimes he'd gone even further than that, but with Gary standing there, Keith would keep things clean and stick to the illusion of protocol.

"It'll only take a second," he told June.

She crossed her arms as if to hide her body from him. "Not you." She pointed at Gary. "I'll only let him do it."

Keith shared a glance with Gary, both men surprised.

"He's not an officer of the law," Keith told June.

"That's one of the reasons I like him more than you, though that's a pretty low bar."

Again, the urge to strike her bubbled in Keith's core. "You—"

"Take it or leave it."

Gary stepped toward her, playing peacemaker. "Okay. It's fine. Let's just get it over with."

June extended her arms and Gary gave her a quick pat down. For not being a cop, he did a decent job of it, but was more respectful of the girl's body than Keith would have been.

"She's clean," Gary said. He looked at June with a sour expression. "You really a groupie?"

She slung the backpack over her shoulders. "I don't give a damn what ya'll call me and sure as hell don't care what ya think of me."

Keith smirked at Gary. "Maybe we oughta let her go out on her own after all if she's so damn star-struck."

Gary shook his head. Keith now perceived him as a man out of his element, one whose time had passed without him even realizing it. Keith would never let that happen to him. He wouldn't allow middle-age to slow and soften him into one of those pathetic, divorced men in their forties who'd blown their chance at a good life. Keith was *single*, not *alone*. He wasn't living with his mother or splitting the rent with another guy. He could get a girl if he wanted to. If the hot ones weren't so pissy and ungrateful, Keith might even settle down. But not a defeated husk of a man like Gary Chatmon. This was one limp private dick. It was more than the twelve-year age difference that set them apart. Keith saw himself as vibrant and cocksure. Gary was depressed and tired. Keith was a new Porsche, Gary a broken laundry machine.

But what does that make Edmund Cox?

Keith had obsessed over the killer's groupies almost as much as they had over Cox. What drew some women—especially fuckable ones—to worship a man who would rape and slaughter them given the chance? The injustice of it was infuriating. Keith could understand why rock stars and movie stars got more pussy than he did, but a serial killer? It made him wish they made the crime scene photos public. Let these feral whores get a good look at what their dream date would really do to them.

Gary seemed to disagree. Keith could tell the man was struggling with what they'd seen in June's backpack, but knew Gary wouldn't let her learn the hard way. He would want to protect her from Cox even if she wanted the killer's knife between her tits. In that sense, he was sticking by June to protect her from herself. He'd gone from private investigator to babysitter. Again, Gary tried to talk Keith and June into going back to the car, and this time they didn't even bother telling him they weren't turning back. They didn't have to. Everyone knew where this was going—where *all three of them* were going.

The river flowed in black ripples, the jagged rocks frothing like the fangs of rabid beasts. The rain had retreated, and the puddles left behind were freezing. Keith liked it cold. It made everything smell so fresh and clean, even a world this decayed.

June started walking again.

Gary held Keith back. "You don't really think she's in cahoots with Cox, do you?"

Keith drew a cigarette from his pack. "Nah. Like I said, Cox works alone. But that don't mean she won't turn on us if she thinks it'll help him."

"She's just a confused kid."

"Hey, we all were at some point, right? But eventually you've gotta call things what they are."

"And what is that?"

Keith grinned. "C'mon, man. Do I really have to spell it out for ya? This chick ain't confused, she's nuts."

They stared at June as she walked on. She hadn't slowed down or looked back. She was heading upriver, with or without them.

"If she's mentally ill," Gary said, "then that's all the more reason to help her."

"Ain't our responsibility."

"*Not our...* Christ, man, you're a *cop*. Isn't helping people your job?"

"You heard her, Chatmon. This is a free country. If she wants to walk around in the woods, she's free to do so."

"But you said it yourself—if Cox gets a hold of her, he'll kill her in the worst way. As far as I'm concerned, we'll be preventing a suicide."

Gary started after June then, jogging along the bank to catch up with her. Keith followed at a leisurely pace, lighting his cigarette, savoring the smoke as night fell in full.

He didn't see June as a threat, but he didn't see her as his burden either.

Keith saw her as one thing only—*bait*.

TWENTY-ONE

AIN'T IT FUNNY, DARLIN'?

The more people I kill, the safer I am. There's beauty in that, I think. Some folks would call it ironic. All those coppers and feds out there huntin' me, lookin' everywheres 'cept where they oughta. They're all led astray by the magic of The River Man, 'cause he's happy with all I done. His blessing is my just reward for the many sweets I've offered up to him. All he wants is for us to be as wicked as he is, and I done proved myself and then some, I'd say.

Folks used to know the power of human sacrifice. In the old days, the Mexicans slaughtered thousands just to celebrate a new temple. Every culture on this earth has shown their love for the gods and ghosts through killing. But somewhere along the way, humans lost sight of what really matters… and what real power is. But I know the truth. I know what brings the biggest reward in life.

It's death.

I suppose you know that now too, darlin'.

See, when I was a boy, all us kids on the river would hunt us up some varmints. Sometimes for eatin', other times just 'cause we was bored. I always liked to make the ones I caught suffer real good. I was just a kittycat toyin' with a rat he done cornered, takin' off one piece at a time. Guess the man don't steer too far from the boy. Some things don't ever change.

It takes the right kind of person to find The River Man. Maybe now,

109

after all I done, it takes the right kind of person to find me too. I think I earned the power of this river, same as he did, and I aim to take every bit of what's coming to me. Just like you came to this valley low to prove your devotion to your man, I have proven myself to The River Man.

Christ wore a crown of thorns.

Mine's made of flesh and bone, and it fits me just right.

***

Edmund paddled on.

The Hollow River flowed around his boat like a million lapping tongues. Rock clusters in the water made for threatening barricades, but he was undeterred. Even the brutal rapids he knew awaited him could not dent his resolve. Let all the fires of Hell rise in a cyclone around his body. He'd gladly burn to get where he was going.

The black walls of sandstone besetting the channel grew higher as he journeyed onward, minerals ripped from this cursed earth to enclose vagrant souls.

Edmund sang to himself. *"I'm just a poor, wayfarin' stranger. Travelin' through this world below."*

His mother had often sung this gospel while collecting eggs in the coop and hacking the heads off chickens. Edmund had always enjoyed watching her slay them, for their decapitated bodies would do a panicked dance before bleeding out. Eventually, Mama made chopping chickens one of his chores, a gift for Edmund's fourth birthday. He'd plucked the eyes out of the first one he killed, cracked its skull open with plyers, and ripped out its nugget of a brain and, curious, tasted it while it was still raw.

"I know dark clouds, will gather 'round me," he sang as he paddled on. *"I know my way, is hard 'n steep."*

The rain-clouds had separated, creating a gorge of darkness in the sky to match the one below, only this one was speckled with stars, the long-traveled light of distant, dead suns. A pale moon cast blue beams upon the surface of the water, causing the river to glimmer in a cryptic ballet.

Edmund reflected upon the flesh-eating bacteria his mother

had suffered when he was twelve, and how he'd had to scrub her back in the washtub. She'd shivered as her rotting flesh fell away with Edmund's every stroke. Her saggy breasts had grown riddled with blisters like extra nipples, and hideous, meaty holes had appeared in her legs. Edmund had to flush them out with bleach to kill the maggots that devoured his mother while she was still alive, but somehow, they always returned. She'd always left her health up to God. Mama considered her deteriorating body "His will" and refused to see doctors.

That's when the dreams had started for Edmund. In them, his mother was on her knees in the mud, her hands tied behind her back as she bent over the chopping block, her head resting on the slab among the offal of countless chickens. She was nude and sopping wet, as if she'd just had her bath, and Edmund came up behind her, also naked, his penis hard and larger than it was in real life. Sores covered it too, mirroring his mother's deteriorating flesh. Instead of the cleaver he used on the chickens, he held the logging axe. When he approached her, she always sang in a high, childlike voice.

"I'm just goin' over Jordan… I'm just goin' over home."

Just as he would swing the axe down upon her neck, Edmund would awake in his cot of burlap and straw in a cold sweat, his britches flooded with his ejaculate. He tried to keep this from happening by masturbating before bed, using the photos Uncle Zeke had given him. They were the ones Zeke had taken in Vietnam; keepsakes of all the rape, torture, and murder he'd inflicted on female villagers and children during the war. Those nude and violated bodies were Edmund's sole source of pornography. At that time, the only other woman he'd ever seen naked was his mother. But while Zeke's pictures always excited young Edmund to the point of orgasm, his wet dreams of beheading Mama continued.

He cared for her as she'd slowly rotted away until she could no longer get out of her cot. Her feet disintegrated. Her fingers snapped off like twigs. Every tooth dropped from her blackened gums and her lips eroded, leaving her swollen, festering tongue to hang out of her mouth. Her eyelids decayed, and the strange disease chewed through her corneas, leaving her blind, mute, and crippled.

Only then did Edmund feel comfortable masturbating in front of her. He did it whenever he bathed her, which he now had to do while she was in bed, scrubbing her down with a wet washcloth, taking his time wiping her withered breasts and cleaning out her vagina while touching himself with his free hand.

In the end, he credited this act with keeping him from decapitating her the way his subconscious mind kept suggesting. He knew what he did was sinful, but whenever shame came creeping, he remembered something Uncle Zeke had told him before being sent to a maximum-security madhouse for the murder of his girlfriend.

"Don't worry 'bout your sinnin'," Zeke had said. "If you don't sin, then it's like Jesus died for nothin'."

Memories of his uncle always made Edmund smile. Now, as he rowed upriver through the cold, dark night, his love for his family warmed him, just as the walls of Mama's insides had kept him warm before he was born into this horrible world.

"*I'm just goin' up that river,*" he sang, "*I'm just goin' over home.*"

TWENTY-TWO

JUNE DIDN'T WANT COMPANY, but she had little choice. The men intended to escort her. The older guy seemed to do it out of chivalry, but the cop's motivation wasn't as forthcoming. He said he was hunting Edmund Cox to bring him to justice, but June got the feeling he was here for something more than that. She only believed about half of what these men said, but that applied to everyone.

She was younger and faster than they were. Plus, it was dark. She could make a break for it. They had guns, but she doubted they would use them on her, especially Gary. And maybe it was better to have them along for the journey. Her run-in with the inbred family had left June rattled. Having bodyguards in this land of deviants was a wise move, even if she hated involving others in her personal business—particularly *this* business.

The strange occurrence in Edmund's shack still shook her. Though she'd not seen the body in the cellar, she'd known it was there, but that was the least of the shack's terrors. The infernal glow and screaming phantoms that had oozed out of the boards left June questioning her sanity. Having others along for her journey would help her discern what horrors were real and what ones were figments of her traumatized brain.

June tolerated her new companions, but that didn't mean she

trusted them. Keith made her skin crawl. She'd dealt with enough abusive pigs to sniff them out with ease. Someone like June even tried to avoid police who weren't blatant bullies. She'd have to watch him closely.

The trio fell quiet as they traveled along the riverbank. Little needed to be said. June wondered if the men felt a similar pull, the sort of driving force that propelled her deeper into the enveloping chasm of the black forest. Their only guide was a sorrowful moon that hung swollen amongst the stars, a baneful, white eye watching with indifference. Mercifully, there was no wind, and their clothes had almost dried, so while the cold made them uncomfortable, they did not risk freezing. The only thing that troubled her was the possibility of having to cross the Hollow River. She didn't know where she was going exactly—none of them did—but the lure within her was leading her upriver like a siren's call. There was a sense of urgency backing it, as if what she sought was fleeing faster than she could pursue.

The melody of the river had become hypnotic. The repetition of the waves gave the gorge a false sense of peace. But the travelers were deep in the hills of a forgotten land where nightmares were made flesh. The modern world could never invade a place like Killen. There would be no phone service, internet access, or emergency services. No law and order, no government. There were only mountain men, derelict women, and their mutant offspring. Twenty-first century Neanderthals sustaining on meth, moonshine, and—in Edmund's case—murder. The only laws of this hinterland were written in blood.

"Hey, look," Keith said.

The others followed his gaze. Ten feet ahead was a small fishing boat that had been beached. There was no dock, and the boat wasn't tied to anything. It appeared abandoned.

They approached it with caution, as if the boat were a trap. Keith looked in all directions like he was scanning for snipers. June squatted beside the boat to get a closer look. The bow was cracked but the damage was high enough on the structure that it wouldn't hinder performance, and there was just enough room for three people.

"I say we take it," June said.

Gary sighed, but Keith spoke before he could. "Good idea."

"We don't know who this belongs too," Gary said.

Keith gestured about the forest. "I don't see anybody 'round here, do you?"

Gary frowned.

"Look," Keith said, "If you're worried you'll get in trouble, don't be. I can always say I took it for official police business. Not that I think anyone is even gonna care we took it." Keith stepped into the boat. "Well, there's no oars, but we've got a motor."

June sat at the bow, noticing dark splatter stains. The boat was empty but for a small tackle box. On top of it, someone had written their name in magic marker.

"*Buzz Fledderjohn*," she read aloud.

The motor was stubborn. Keith yanked the chord several times, cursing at it to start. When the motor finally belched to life, Gary took a deep breath and climbed aboard, sitting between the others.

"Can't believe I'm doing this," he said. "I must've lost my damned mind."

Join the club, June thought.

The boat entered the river, a needle going into a vein. The motor sounded like a chainsaw. June wondered if Edmund had ever used one on a victim. She couldn't remember reading anything about him doing so, but the authorities believed he'd killed more people than they knew of. Given his affinity for dismemberment, a chainsaw seemed like an obvious choice. June had a sudden mental image of Edmund Cox revving a STIHL, his bare chest caked in gore, the screams of the dying putting a smile on his haggard face. It was a vision lifted from horror films, but it packed more punch because the slasher was real.

A voice made her turn her head. She'd thought it was Gary speaking, but he was silently watching the river. The voice returned, whispering over the rumble of the motorboat, somehow sounding like it came from the woods beyond the shore and yet right in her ear at the same time.

"Your mother never had the opportunities you do," the voice said.

A chill went through June.

Grandpa?

It'd been so long since she'd heard him speak, but a family member's voice never truly faded from the mind. She'd heard him say these same words before, back when she was still living at home. June had been only fifteen then, but she'd already caused her grandparents a great deal of concern. They knew she'd been running around with older boys, sneaking out at night to get high on whatever drugs were available, and having sex in the beds of pickup trucks, sometimes with multiple partners.

"Your grandfather's right," Gramma had told June. "Your poor mother was only fourteen when she had you. She never got the opportunities you have now, June."

"She not my mother," she'd sharply replied. "She's just a zombie."

Her grandfather had slapped the table. "Don't you *ever* talk about your mother like that, young lady! You don't understand what she went thro—"

June had risen from the table then, sick of her grandparents' lectures. That night, she'd tried two new rebellions—crack cocaine and sex with a woman. Not a teenage girl, but a woman in her early forties who was the mother of one of her school friends. June couldn't remember her name now. All she remembered was the sweet escape the mix of sex and drugs had offered her, a temporary reprieve from the suffocating depression of her everyday world.

Sitting in the boat now, her grandmother's voice whispered in her ear, raising the hairs at the back of June's neck.

"*Why are you doing this?*" Gramma asked.

June flinched. She turned in every direction, her heart racing. She looked back at the men, but they were no longer there. Her grandparents had replaced them.

Grandpa was at the stern of the boat. Even in the darkness, June saw his face was awash in blood so dark it was purple. His suit was soaked with it. Gramma sat in the middle of the boat, giving June a closer look at her damage. The old woman's face was charred on the left side. The right was missing completely, her skull a half moon of gore. She reached for June with bloody fingers, and June shut her eyes tight and screamed.

"June?"

A hand was on her arm. She tugged, but the grip held. *This is it,* she thought. *You're being dragged down to Hell.*

But when she opened her eyes, it was only Gary Chatmon looking at her with concern. Behind him, the cop was glaring at her. June's grandparents had vanished like smoke.

"June?" Gary asked again. "Are you okay?"

Her mouth was so dry she struggled to speak. "Yeah. Yeah, sorry."

Gary stared at her, so she offered the best lie she could think of. "Dozed off for a sec. Had a bad dream is all."

He exhaled. "Christ, you scared the hell out of me."

You think you're scared?

June sniffed back tears, hoping the men couldn't see them in the dark. She gazed over the murky current, looking for something but not knowing what. Ghosts? Illusions? Any explanation as to what was happening here? She watched the Killen woods roll on, a dense thicket as black and loveless as the furthest reaches of space, and though she saw no movement within its shadows, she felt certain they were no longer alone.

TWENTY-THREE

KEITH CAUGHT HIMSELF THINKING about the Josh
Negus shooting again. Trying to take his mind off it, he lit a
cigarette and focused on the river ahead. It looked like thousands of panels of smoked glass. Some time had passed since
he'd operated a motorboat. It should have brought back memories of happier times on the lake, back when he was a teenager
and young girls still wanted to fuck him. Those summers had
seemed to last forever. Now the season raced by faster every
year. Instead of spending summers waterskiing and getting
drunk around a campfire with friends, he lost them to the job,
investigating one heinous act after another until the entire human race seemed suspicious. His life had become one big doom
scroll. Was it any wonder he longed to escape back to his youth
by diving between a teenager's thighs?

The one in this boat would do.

How easy would it be for Keith to shoot Gary in the back,
toss him overboard, and take what he wanted from June—what
he *fucking deserved*? It was only a dark fantasy, but it kept him
from replaying the Negus shooting in his head. He imagined the
look of shock on June's face becoming one of desire. Keith's
boldness would impress her, how he took what he wanted even
at the cost of a human life. Halfway through raping her, she'd

start to enjoy it. He would show her what it was like to get fucked by a real man instead of the scrawny, young wimps she probably put out for. He wondered how many cocks she'd sucked and if she'd ever taken it in the ass, if she liked to be tied up or choked at the moment of climax. Not that he cared what she wanted. It was *his* desires that would take precedent. Just the thought of introducing her to his perverted inner world was enough to stir his lust.

When she'd suddenly screamed, Keith got hard. He crossed his legs to hide it from the others. June said she'd fallen asleep sitting up and had a little nightmare. *How cute.* Here she was in the middle of nowhere, chasing a serial killer who would do far worse things to her than Keith ever would, and yet it was her dreams that freaked her out and not her present situation? He'd been right in his assessment of her. June was fucked in the head.

Aren't they all?

He'd been so eager to graduate from a uniformed officer to a plainclothes detective, but now that he was no longer on patrol, Keith found there were things he missed about it. Pulling young women over in rural areas was one of them. He'd never gotten so many blowjobs before or since. All he'd have to find was a little weed or some molly. He'd turn off his body camera, and then the negotiations would begin.

It wasn't like he raped the girls. He always gave them a choice—suck it or go to jail. He was so successful in getting what he wanted from them he'd started staking out places where teenage girls gathered—shopping plazas, concert halls, the boardwalk—and would wait for a group to load into a car and then follow them, pulling them over in a park or an empty side road. If there were boys too, Keith would rough them up, both to keep them from resisting and show their girlfriends he meant business.

One time while on night duty, he'd hit pay-dirt when he discovered a car parked near the baseball field around one in the morning. Inside, two kids were necking, and were so wrapped up in it they hadn't noticed Keith approach until he turned the flashlight on them and knocked on the window. The girl's shirt was unbuttoned, and she covered her tiny breasts. In the flash-light's beam, her braces glimmered like a wishing well. The boy's learner's permit said he was sixteen. The girl told Keith she was fifteen. Though Keith had no cause to search them or the car, he did it anyway, finding a rubber in the boy's coat pocket and half a sheet of acid in the glove-box.

"This is enough to count as intent to sell," Keith told them. "That's a felony charge."

The boy's voice trembled even worse than his limbs. "Please... I-I wasn't gonna sell it. It's for a party next week. For me and m-m-my friends. That's all."

"There's about fifty tabs of acid here," Keith said, having lined the kids up with their hands on the hood of the car, legs spread. "That's enough to send you both away for a long time."

The boy immediately said, "She has nothing to do with this."

Keith admired his effort to save his girlfriend, so he tested just how far she would go to save her boyfriend in return. Doing a pat down, he slid his hand between the girl's legs and rubbed her crotch over her jeans. She trembled as he pressed against her, but said nothing, so he put his arms around her waist and undid her fly.

"Hey!" the boy shouted, rising from the hood. "You can't—"

Keith knocked him back onto the hood. "I didn't say you could move!"

"Please, just leave u—"

Keith drew his baton and cracked the kid behind the knees, dropping him. The girl shrieked, and Keith shoved her forward, bending her over the car, his hand pressing her face into the hood. That's when he whispered her options to her.

This would become one of Keith's fondest memories. He liked to think he took the virginity that had been promised to the boyfriend that very night. The kid was as stupid as he was chivalrous and tried to stop his girlfriend from giving in, so Keith cuffed and beat him a little until the girl was begging Keith to stop, promising she'd be obedient. She'd been a *very* good girl that night, despite all her blubbering. As for the boyfriend, Keith was kind enough to destroy the evidence by making the kid eat the entire half sheet of LSD.

The kid was never the same after that. He had several petty run-ins with the law in the years that followed, and Keith saw him at the station from time to time, his limbs always twitchy, speech garbled even when sober, his eyes like Rasputin's. Keith didn't know what became of the girl. He liked to think he'd taught her a valuable lesson. If the experience had put her in a permanent dark place, it was none of his concern. A deal was a deal, and she'd made her choice.

Rarely did people file complaints against him, but usually the ones who did were the ones he'd arrested, not allowed to go free in exchange for sexual favors. And complaints happened with a lot of cops. Citizens loved to cry foul when they were placed behind bars, so warranted complaints were often grouped with the phony or exaggerated ones. Cops protected other cops. Keith had an impeccable reputation with his colleagues and his record with the department was one of unwavering dedication, so the complaints against him were always swept under the rug, and the times he truly abused his power weren't reported at all because he'd so thoroughly intimidated his young victims. The worst punishment Keith had ever faced was a lecture from the chief on how to avoid being charged with harassment. And as he'd moved up, he'd gotten more careful.

It wasn't until the shooting of Josh Negus that he was put on any kind of leave.

You're thinking about it again.

But how could he not? Even though Keith was out here to take down Edmund Cox, there was a macabre energy to the Killen countryside that kept pulling him back into his existential void, like stones in the pockets of a sinking man. He'd been feeling it since they'd come across that mutilated couple, a dark force that rerouted his mind to memories of pain and perversion.

You had it coming, Negus.

The haunted eyes of the little girl returned to Keith, and when he blinked against the thought the image of those eyes remained when he opened his own, two grief-stricken orbs hovering in the blackness before fading like their hope for the future. Keith knew a lot about hopelessness. He'd learned a long time ago that the only genuine hope was false hope, and the only real luck was bad. There was no code to which he subscribed. Even his allegiance to the police force was a sort of act designed to keep him in a position of power, the only thing that thrilled him anymore. For Keith Drakeson, there was no moral creed to live by, only an endless quest for self-gratification at the expense of others. Life was a pointless parade of lust, greed, and violence. There was no true meaning, no honest religion, no believable gods.

And there was no such thing as *ghosts*.

There was no River Man any more than there was an Easter Bunny. He was just another Bigfoot, these hillbillies' version of alien abduction stories. Edmund's shack might be an abode of horrors, but the only haunted house was that of the human mind, a collection of traumatized nerve endings that flickered with the most abhorrent snapshots of its past.

As they continued their journey, Keith looked up at the swollen face of the moon and imagined it slowly drawing closer to the earth until a collision was eminent. Those final days would show the true nature of mankind. All the humanity people were so proud of would disappear like steam after a summer storm, leaving behind the true face of a failed species, slick with blood and tears. Keith longed to see society stripped down in such a way, so he could prove all people were as corrupt as he was, if not worse.

Edmund Cox was certainly worse.

Josh Negus had been too, hadn't he?

TWENTY-FOUR

THE WATER WAS CHANGING.

Gary had noticed the Hollow River's bizarre colors by day, how the currents ran a forest green at some points, and nearly black in others, fluctuating in drab shades of ruin. The coming of night had locked in the river's darkness, turning it the color of hot tar, the moonlight making the surface glimmer like wet leather. Now that they were on the river, Gary could see the waves up close, and how they moved less fluidly the further they ventured. The water had grown sludgy. It emitted a sharp odor. It wasn't the swampy smell so common to southern bodies of water, like the sulfurous fart stench that permeated all of Georgia, but a stink so hefty it bordered on an assault.

Putting out his hand, Gary dipped two fingers into the river. Its touch was arctic, stinging his tissue down to the bone. When he drew his fingers out, a brackish ooze came with them, clinging to him with the consistency of aloe vera or semen, only black as ink.

"What the hell?" he said to himself.

June looked back at him with no expression, showing all the emotion of a department store mannequin. Before he could say anything, she turned away again, staring at the river ahead and the deep embrace of the gorge.

Gary stared at it too. The limestone walls that beset them had grown higher, the dead trees raking against the backdrop of the stars like the desperate claws of an earth trying to drag itself out of the sun's orbit. How high above sea level were those jagged cliffs? How deep into this uncharted wilderness had they traveled? How many miles in every direction were they from the civilized world? How far was he from home?

Home.

Such a novel idea. But what was a home without family? How could a home exist without proper love to fill it? Gary had given up on the concept, just as he'd given up on every other milestone that was supposed to come with a man's life. There would be no next stage, only a sad continuation of this gray oblivion until he found the serenity of the grave. His wife was dead, and their only child had been murdered in her belly. Gary liked to think they were at peace. He was the one who'd ended up in Hell.

Gary didn't date or try to find someone new. He didn't hold out hope to have a baby with another woman. He didn't even put effort into improving himself, so he'd be more attractive to the opposite sex. Any woman who showed interest in him was highly suspect. Gary didn't trust them. And whenever a woman managed to break through his wall and get close to him, Gary pushed her away because he didn't want them to suffer through the ordeal of caring about him. He believed women deserved better than that. To drag anyone else into his vortex of constant suffering would be a crime he could never forgive himself for.

Gary Chatmon was more alone than he'd ever been. They said it was better to have loved and lost than to have never loved at all, but Gary doubted that, at least in his case. Was it really better to have all he'd ever loved taken from him in a hail of bullets than it would have been to never have met Lacy?

Home.

The rotting shacks on this river were more *home* than he would ever know again. The hill folk might be strange, but they had families in their ramshackle cabins. Still, there were other loners out in these sticks. Gary wondered if he could commit to an eremitical lifestyle the way these mountain hermits had, if he could live off the land without electricity or running water, catching his dinner with fishing poles and a double-barrel shotgun. He could spend his nights reading the great Russian novels by candlelight. It was a romantic thought but held little resemblance to reality. He was far more likely to go mad out here, just as the locals seemed to have, and end up wandering around singing like that crazy preacher or doing what Edmund Cox had...

Gary stopped the thought.

No. You could never be like Edmund Cox. You might go mad out here, but you'd never rip out people's guts and have sex with their severed heads.

There were limits to Gary's poor mental health. It wasn't homicide that beckoned him, but suicide. It ran circles around his other thoughts, hiding in the cobwebs of his mind only to reappear in random games of peekaboo. Even when the urge was subdued, it was still there, its lulling call reminding him there was always a way out of this. It danced around each effort to up his serotonin, overpowering every brand of anti-depressants and mood stabilizers medical science could offer. Suicide was his one true relief, the last-ditch hope for stillness.

Lacy would have wanted him to move on. Gary knew that. She would have hated to see what he'd become since her murder, and that just made him hate himself more. Even now he was failing her, just like he'd failed to keep her and the baby safe. If only he'd been a better provider, Lacy wouldn't have had to keep working while pregnant and wouldn't have been at the school that day. Everyone told him there was nothing he could have done, that he shouldn't blame himself for their deaths, and though he knew this to be true, it did nothing to stop him from clinging to that guilt. Like a stubborn dog, he'd sunk his teeth in and refused to let go.

Gary sighed as he wiped the slime from his hand.

How long had they been out here? Why was he out here in the first place? Roaming the woods in search of Jessica Hong's body was ridiculous enough, but now he was in a stolen boat with two other damaged souls, going deeper into the heart of nowhere with no plan and no clear way home.

Home.

Was that what kept him out here? That he had nowhere else to go? No one was waiting for him. He didn't even have a pet. Who would notice if he never came back? Gary often went days without talking to another human being. He expected to die like some old cat lady, the police breaking his door down weeks after his demise after being called by neighbors to address the stench of death.

Gary tensed at the thought. *The stench of death.*

That's what the river's smell reminded him of. It wasn't the fishy odor some rivers had, but the pungent reek of a carcass.

A large mouse had once died inside the walls of he and Lacy's house, causing that stink to bleed into everything they owned. It had forced Gary to break into the wall with a hammer to get the body out. Lacy had washed their clothes twice before deciding to replace everything. That smell had been dreadful, but the stink of human decay was even worse.

Gary didn't see a lot of dead bodies. He was a private investigator, not a cop. But one missing person's case had led him to a corpse. The young man was a drug addict and had overdosed in his car in the parking lot of an abandoned strip mall. It was summer, and his body had cooked in the heat, bloating and putrefying. The smell was so awful Gary had literally followed his nose to the corpse after receiving a tip that the young man often parked back there to sleep or shoot up. It was the first dead body he'd seen up close. The second was when he'd had to identify his wife at the morgue. Officials had warned Gary that he *really* didn't want to see her in the shape her body was in after the shooting, but he'd insisted. He would spend the rest of his life wishing he'd listened to those officials instead.

The odor on the river was like that of the swollen junkie in that hot car, only fainter. Gary sensed the further they went upriver, the stronger the death fetor would grow, much like when he'd taken each additional step toward that car. He almost asked the others if they smelled it too but decided against it. What did it matter if they smelled it or not?

Neither of them could be deterred. Keith wanted to get his man. And June... well, Gary wasn't sure what June was after, and the more he observed her, the less he wanted to. The girl wore a preternatural aura about her like a second skin. It was as if she were another species, like a pod-person from a science-fiction film. There was a blankness to her that Gary found chilling, and the girl's youth made her deadness even more disturbing.

Gary looked at her from behind. Her long hair fluttered in the breeze, black as crow feathers. As she gazed across the water, her pale face was in silhouette against the moon, searching for whatever secret had brought her to the Hollow River. In a place like this, all secrets were dark, all silence incriminating. Did June worship Edmund the way Keith suggested? Could she really lust after such unquestionable evil? Though she seemed odd, it was hard to imagine her fawning over a serial killer. But that probably applied to any groupies of murderers. No one expected their daughter to grow up to crush on the next Ted Bundy.

There was only one question that mattered now: *could they trust her?*

But this brought another chilling question: *could Gary trust Keith?*

He almost turned around to look at the cop, but a strange sense of dread slithered about Gary's bones. He had the weird feeling that if he turned around, Keith would be holding his pistol, and it would be the last thing Gary saw. Though he had no basis for this scenario, in that moment, Gary accepted it as an absolute certainty. So instead, he watched June at the bow, her profile like a cherub's, her greasy hair moving like the curling legs of a dying black widow.

Her lips parted as the moon filled with blood.

The blue light gave way to a transitional purple, and then the world turned burgundy. The redness was bright enough to reveal the river and the surrounding woods, the moon now a crimson sun. Gary gasped, blinking rapidly at what he hoped was an illusion, a trick of the brain rather than a trick of reality itself. It was as if they'd entered another dimension, a hellscape of coral rock and broken trees where a claret river flowed like the blood of dead gods. What wasn't red was black—the encompassing gorge, the shadows of the thicket, the returning thunderclouds. The redness made grim adumbrations of the world they'd left behind, like the faint image of distant mountains on a smoky horizon. It contorted the features of the known universe into grotesque aberrations, as if the world had shattered and been glued back together, a model forged by a violent hand.

Gary's heart fell into his stomach. His mouth opened, but no sound escaped him. If the others noticed the land's transformation, they had no reaction. They seemed frozen, as if…

As if stricken with rigor mortis.

Gary's nostrils filled with the foul stench of corpses. Though the smell had grown overpowering, it wasn't what brought tears to his eyes.

Towering walls of rock on either side of the river had shifted, mutating their form. The stone cracked like thunder, every snapping slate having a different tone. They became musical but distorted, each new crack in the limestone producing another strum like the plucked strings of an electric guitar. The sound was sloppy and garbled, a bluesy dirge muddied by a heavy tone, like a guitar's output through a blown amplifier. A crazed, acoustic slide guitar underlined this black requiem, followed by a hushed percussion like chains being dragged across concrete. A raspy baritone carried through the gorge, sounding half man and half beast, mewling like an Alaskan Husky yet serenading like a gospel hymn.

As the walls crumbled, something took form in their place.

Gary peered at the shiny, metal boxes. They were six foot tall and lined up in endless rows, little padlocks keeping their contents secure.

Lockers, Gary realized, unable to breathe.

The river of blood now covered a tile floor. The hallway wound through the lockers just as the Hollow River had wound through the Killen woods, gleaming red and wet as the percussion became the staccato of gunshots. Gary flinched, and with each blast another little body rose out of the blood like a dead man floating in a pool. The children drifted in their own gore, their exit wounds steaming in the arctic air. Another pluck of the droning guitar, and all the lockers came open, revealing dead kids propped inside them as if they were coffins. An ill wind blew, carrying the smell of human rot, and blowing dead leaves crackled like embers as they scattered through this hall of Hell.

At the end of the hallway stood Lacy. She stared at Gary, then started toward him. Horror closed his throat. He couldn't move or speak or look away no matter how hard he desired to. His dead wife drew closer, the river of blood parting before her as if she were Moses, sousing the bodies of slain children as they continued to stack.

Tears burned down Gary's cheeks. Lacy looked as he'd last seen her, a bullet hole just below her right eye where her cheekbone had caved in. Only this time the wounds were fresh. Blood dribbled from her head's every orifice and seeped through her blouse. She fingered the buttons, then slipped her hand through and tore the shirt open, revealing the additional bullet wounds in her swollen belly.

"I love you, Gary," she said through a mouthful of blood.

Lacy dug into the holes in her belly with both hands, ripping the tissue apart. Blood left her cavity in a crimson waterfall, sounding like a rushing river.

"No!" Lacy cried. "My baby! *Please, my baby!*"

Gary wept as his wife reached into her open womb and pulled out the tiny skeleton.

It opened its mouth and screamed.

TWENTY-FIVE

I DREAM OF DEAD WOMEN.

I carry those I killed inside me, almost like I'd swallowed 'em. A soul eater. They share my blood now, just like when I was a kid and me and my buddies would cut our palms open and shake hands, makin' us blood brothers.

There's a heaviness that comes with bein' a killer, darlin'. The hearts of all you murder live inside you forever, swimmin' in your mind like tadpoles that can scream. I hear 'em in the night, callin' my name from their tombs. Sometimes they whisper like crickets. Other times they screech like falcons on fire. And all over again, I can smell their innards and taste their pretty cunts. I kill 'em over and over, and the blood runs like the river, takin' me back into that sweet, red world of nightmares and pain.

Sometimes I dream while I'm awake. Shrinks call that madness, but I call it enlightenment. *Learned that there word from a college student by the name of Jessica. She was a Chinese, and they worship Buddha. Enlightenment's what them Buddhists work their whole lives to get to, and most of 'em never find it. That's 'cause they don't know what I know. That girl was tryin' to find out. She wanted to learn more 'bout The River Man. I showed her all she needed to know. 'Bout him. 'Bout me. And then, she showed you, darlin'. You came for the key, and she done gave it to ya, didn't she? Gave it right from her heart and you ripped it from 'tween her ribs.*

But I didn't show you the way, Lori.

130

You showed yourself.

***

The cliff jutted over the river in the shape of a sickle. Edmund gazed upon it, looking for The River Man's shack. He couldn't see it yet and didn't detect any smoke, but the moon had turned pink, and the stars were burning red. Soon all the world would glow that color, as if all of Killen were one massive open wound. In a way, Edmund figured it was.

The River Man's realm had multiple doorways that opened at different intervals for different people. No two experiences were alike. For some, the redness began the moment they reached the Hollow River. For others, it only existed at the cursed threshold of The River Man's shack. Edmund longed for the savory kiss of that redness, the way it opened the gates of one's consciousness like a powerful drug and set every inner horror loose. But he could be patient, and for The River Man, he would even be respectful. This was *his* universe. Edmund was just a wayfaring stranger, wandering through this world below.

For now, he thought with a smirk.

He paddled on through the tarry waves, pleased to see them fade from black to the dark purple color of human organs. Every time the oars rose out of the water, they dribbled redder. In his pocket, the key forged of his darlings grew warm. Edmund assured them with a little lover's pat. The current increased, and the rowboat picked up speed. Rounding a bend in the river, the rapids appeared before Edmund in a rising froth, the foam gathering around onyx rocks that jutted skyward like the black horns of a giant. He stroked on, undeterred, a grin distorting his features like a funhouse mirror.

The water blushed like vomited wine. Clumps of black hair drifted in the blood, a reminder of all the times he'd yanked his victims' hair from their heads. Other pieces floated by—severed fingers, toes, tongues, and breasts, all bobbing on the surface of a steady stream of gore. There was a persistent hissing sound as steam rose from the current, setting Edmund's body hair on end. His extremities tingled and he wet his lips, tasting copper upon the air as he proceeded along the river of flesh, surrounded by the many scraps of his darlings.

The new key burned against his thigh, a response to the presence of its sisters. Edmund reached into his other pocket for Lori's eye and unwrapped it to reveal to her the crimson dimension.

"We're back in that belly of the beast now, darlin'. This here's where you done really proved your love for me. I know it. I feel it in my veins, like the sweetest disease."

Edmund gritted his teeth as the current took him, the trip becoming a white-water rafting adventure at the bend in the river. Waves of blood splashed against his skin, the boat sprinkled with slivers of sinew and a hail of bone shards. The boat hit something—*hard*—but continued onward. Edmund's every muscle flexed but his heart rate never sped up. His serene smile remained as the rowboat burst through the blood rapids, narrowly missing the crags. A cyclone of dead leaves whirled about him, blackening a magenta sky like a horde of locusts. He smelled wet metal and burning flesh, heard demonic laughter and the screams of young women begging him for their lives.

Suddenly the redness was all-encompassing.

"This is where I belong," Edmund said. "Now and forever."

An intense sensation of power riveted him. He felt as weightless as a ghost. A carefree aloofness he'd not felt since childhood returned to him, and he laughed so hard he cried.

Edmund saw something caught within a cluster of rocks near the riverbank. Getting closer, he realized it was a corpse. It had bloated, and the fish, buzzards, and insects had been picking at it, but Edmund could still tell it was an old, black man. Here the waters calmed, so he paddled toward the splayed carcass. The boat had cracked in the rapids and was taking on water now. Edmund saw the man's head was split open, and someone had sawed one foot off just above the ankle.

A fine offering, Edmund thought.

A severed foot could serve the same purpose as his collection of lady parts.

Can't go to The River Man empty-handed.

He wondered if Lori had made this sacrifice or if some other traveler had taken the old man's life. The River Man was never shy of visitors, even if most of them turned back screaming when they got too close. As Edmund admired the gruesome handiwork, a curl of black fog wafted out of the thicket, causing him to look up.

Between the rows of willow trees was a thin trail. Smoke moved down the hillside in a tenebrous waterfall, smelling of charred flesh.

Edmund smiled at the dead man. Worms danced in the corpse's hollowed eye sockets, and the maggot-eaten mouth revealed jack-o'-lantern teeth that appeared to smile back at Edmund, welcoming him. Docking the boat upon the bank, Edmund stepped onto the cursed earth and stared up the long trail ahead, a passageway to cosmos of delectable horrors.

He held up Lori's eye to show her all they'd accomplished. "Honey, I'm home."

Edmund Cox started his climb to The River Man's lair.

TWENTY-SIX

THEY KEPT THE MONEY IN A LOCKBOX.
June had seen her grandfather with it, stashing the day's take from the bait and tackle shop when he came home. Only he and Gramma knew the combination. Gramma went into the lockbox for grocery money and other household expenses, but otherwise left it in their bedroom cabinet along with her jewelry and other valuables, preferring to be frugal. If June could just get into that box on a Sunday, after Grandpa had stuffed it with a full week's earnings, she'd have enough cash to get out of this stinking town for good.

Despite everything they tried to tell her, she wasn't a kid anymore. June was sick of this jerkwater burg and wanted out so she could see what the rest of America had to offer. She wanted to go to the desert, see New England foliage, and visit the Pacific Ocean. She wanted new friends, new men, new parties. Having no car wasn't an issue. June was a pretty, teenage girl. Rides would be easy. All she needed was a nest egg to cover the cost of motel rooms and food when she couldn't mooch off some horn-dog guy in his forties. She'd learned at an early age just how susceptible middle-aged men were to the flirtations of a pigtailed teen.

There had to be several grand in that lockbox. Grandpa's bait and tackle shop was no goldmine—nothing in Killen was—but he and Gramma were miserly, pinching pennies as if it were The Great Depression. They had a checking account, but Grandpa distrusted the banks and liked to keep plenty of cash on hand. It wouldn't have surprised June if he kept bricks of money hidden in the walls. If he did, her grandparents could keep it. June was fair. She only wanted what was in the box. Then she would be out of their hair forever, and out of Killen at last. She was sick of feeling like a burden, and even sicker of being told what to do all the time—who she could hang out with, where she could go, and when she had to be home. No drugs or alcohol or even cigarettes, and definitely *no sex*.

"Not while you're under my roof," Grandpa always said.

June was about to make the old fart eat those words.

The best time to make the steal would be while her grandparents were at Sunday mass. The only problem was they always insisted she go with them, that she needed God in her life. June didn't believe in any of that. If God's love had given her a disturbed mother and absent father, it was *He* who had to ask *June* for forgiveness, not the other way around. Churchgoing was another rule set in stone in her grandparent's house, but as she'd entered her teens, June had freed herself from the pinions of piety. Her indoctrination into the Christian faith lost its hold as all the horrors and injustices of the world grew clearer in her maturing mind. So, June had tried to argue against her grandparents' insistence she tag along to worship *their* God. She claimed to want to find her own spiritual path. Though she had no interest in religion of any kind, she thought this would be a viable method of getting out of church. But her grandfather wasn't liberal minded enough to accept June's desire for theological exploration. It was one of many wedges that had been driving them further apart.

To skip church, she'd have to be incapable of going.

Early Sunday morning, while it was still dark, June tiptoed into the kitchen, opened a can of vegetable soup, and brought it to the bathroom, which was beside her grandparent's bedroom. She made loud retching noises until she heard footfalls, then dumped the soup into the toilet and discarded the can in the trash bin, concealing it with wads of toilet paper.

There was a knock at the door.

"June bug?" Gramma asked. "You okay in there?"

June had left the door unlocked. She didn't reply to her grandmother, giving a silent invite for her to come in. When she did, June looked up at her with drool hanging from her lip, then retched over the bowl again.

"Oh, my heavens," Gramma said, coming to June and patting her back. "Just get it all out, honey."

Now June had not just an excuse, but also a witness. When it came time for church, she got the pass she'd been hoping for and was left alone in the house—alone with the cashbox. She entered her grandparent's bedroom the moment their car disappeared down the street. The cabinet was closed. When she tried the handle, she found it locked. That they didn't trust her angered June, even though she was proving their point. She went out to the tool shed for a screwdriver and shoved it between the cabinet's handles, like a crowbar. The doors wouldn't budge.

"Fuck you," June hissed.

She'd been trying to open the cabinet without ruining it. But it didn't matter anymore. She was never coming back here and would never have to face her grandparents after what she'd done. Down the hall, June went to the gun cabinet in the living room. It too was locked, but its doors were glass, so she threw the screwdriver through one and reached in to undo the latch. The doors swung open. Grandpa was a hunter and had often taken June into the woods to catch game. He had two long rifles and one pump-action shotgun. She'd been taught how to use all three. She grabbed the latter, knowing her grandfather always kept it loaded in case of intruders. Bringing the shotgun to the master bedroom, she took aim at the cabinet and fired, bursting the hickory hatchway into splinters. They swung open like saloon doors.

June's ears rang. She hadn't been ready for the loudness of the blast. It was a good thing they had no close neighbors. Grabbing the cashbox, she spied her grandmother's diamond ring and pearl necklace. She reached for them, then reconsidered and let them be.

The goddamned cashbox was locked too.

"Shit."

At least it was a small, flimsy key lock on a latch. It would be easy to break, which defeated the purpose of it. Still carrying the shotgun, June brought the box to the kitchen table, drew a butcher knife from the block, and wedged it into the gap to pry the box open. The lock held. June huffed. She didn't want to blast the box open and damage any of the cash inside. Deciding to return to the shed for a new tool, June spun around and saw the casserole dish on the counter, wrapped in foil.

Her breath caught in her chest. Gramma often made these dishes for Reverend Lawrence.

She forgot it, June realized.

A shadow moved behind her, and June spun to see her grandparents standing in the kitchen entryway. With her ears still ringing from the shotgun blast, she hadn't heard them return home for the dish. Her grandmother had gone pale with shock, but her grandfather was red as an apple. They looked at the cashbox, then the shotgun in June's hands. On the floor behind them lay the shattered glass of the gun cabinet.

"I don't believe it," Grandpa said. "I just don't believe it. After all we've done for you…"

Gramma began to cry.

"Look what ya done to your poor Nana," Grandpa said. "Have ya no decency, girl?"

June swallowed hard but remained stoic. "Guess not."

Grandpa shook his head. "There's a demon in you. I've tried to deny it, tried to wish it weren't so. But every day it's become more clear to see. The evil's in your blood and The Devil's in your ear."

Gramma wept. "No… Harold, don't say that."

"We can't ignore it no more, Gloria. Our June is full of sin. Just like—"

"Harold!"

June shouted over them. "Now look! I'm gettin' outta this

place. *For good.* So just get outta my way."

"Like hell, I will," Grandpa said, wagging his finger. "I'll be damned if Imma let ya steal from your Nana and me."

June sneered. "Well then, I guess you're damned."

Shaking with anger, Grandpa came at June. He'd rarely struck her—once when he'd caught her in her room with a boy performing oral sex on her, and once when she'd stolen the family car and hit a tree—but June knew he aimed to hit her now. She raised the shotgun. She didn't intend to use it, but she didn't intend to be smacked either. Tired of her grandfather's authority, June was prepared to demand respect.

But she did not intimidate her grandfather. He reached for the barrel of the gun. They struggled. Grandpa was strong, and June was just a small teenage girl.

"June!" Gramma cried. "Why're you doing this?"

June felt the shotgun slipping away from her. She couldn't let that happen. Without thinking it through, she put her finger against the trigger, believing a warning shot would shock the old man into submission. Instead, the blast went over her grandfather's shoulder and took half her grandmother's face away.

The old woman's head jerked back in a burst of blood and bone, decorating the cabinets. She stood there, suspended in space, and then her body gave out at the knees, and she crumbled like a discarded doll.

Grandpa screamed. "Gloria!"

When he turned to go to Gramma, June noticed blood coming out of his ear. Though the proximity of the blast had ruptured his eardrum, his only concern was his wife. June stood there in silent awe of what had happened. One tap of a trigger and her grandmother was no more. It'd been so terribly easy.

June hadn't intended things to go this far. Or had she?

She shook the thought from her head as tears filled her eyes, but she didn't know whether to cry or laugh. Her world had collapsed into gruesome absurdity. The only way out of the madness was to charge straight through it.

"Gloria!" Grandpa cried, scooping his dead wife in his arms. Her neck was limp, and when her head tilted back it released its contents onto the tile. Grandpa clutched her corpse to him, her blood drenching him and staining his face as he hung his head and wept. June had never seen her grandfather cry before, and something about seeing it now disgusted her.

"You're inhuman!" he shouted at her.

June's chest quaked, her heart ready to burst.

"I shoulda listened to your mother," Grandpa said. "She wanted to get rid of you."

June's palms sweated as she gripped the shotgun harder.

"You'll pay for this," Grandpa said. "*Murderer*! I'll see to it you're tried as an adult. I hope ya rot in jail! You're dead to me, June! You understand? You're *dead to me*."

His words devolved into blubbering, and he bent over his wife's body again.

June blinked the tears from her eyes but did not sob or make a sound. She felt like a sleepwalker who'd just been rattled awake to find themselves in a strange place they'd never been before. Everything was alien. It disturbed her until she realized that made everything *new*.

Isn't that what you wanted?

The new world lay before her, open and fresh, waving her in. All she had to do now was accept the invitation and leave no trace of her former life behind.

Grandpa snarled at her a final time. "You're dead to me!"

She raised the shotgun. "You're dead to me too."

***

Thunder shook June out of the memory.

The moon was a normal color again, but an army of clouds had gathered over the river. Pink lightning wormed through them like veins, brightening the gorge in brilliant flashes.

"Storm's comin'," Keith said.

Gary suddenly jolted. He breathed deep as if he'd just emerged from the depths of the ocean. His eyes were bloodshot, and he bore the look of a wild animal, ready to fight or flee.

"No," he cried. "No, Lacy. No, *no*!"

"Gary?" Keith said.

Keith reached for him, but Gary shook him loose.

"My wife," Gary said. "You have to let me in, *my wife* is in there!"

"What're you talking about?"

"The school! She's a teacher here... she... she..."

June watched as Gary slowly returned to his senses. He looked in every direction. He seemed surprised to be where he was—a small boat on a river at night. June supposed it should surprise them all they were here. Gary breathed heavily, clutching his chest like a man having a heart attack.

"Are you alright?" June asked.

Elbows on his knees, Gary hunched over and shook his head. "What... what is happening?"

Keith drew his cigarettes and offered one to Gary, which he refused.

"You must've dozed off too," Keith said. "Another bad dream, right?" He chuckled. "I'd better watch out. I must be next."

June tensed. Had Gary experienced a hallucination like the one she'd had of her grandparents' corpses being in the boat with her?

"Gary," she said, "did you see something?"

Gary looked up at her as if noticing her presence for the first time.

"What did you see?" June asked. "Did you have, like, a vision?"

The last remaining moonbeam fell upon Gary like a spotlight in a darkened theater. He looked so much older in that moment, as if being on the river was draining him. Perhaps it was.

"I think," he began, "think I... I..."

She took his hand, surprising them both. "Your wife?"

His eyes glazed. He looked away and rubbed them with his sleeve.

"Hey," June said. "What about your wife?"

Gary shook his head. "I don't know what it was. Maybe I did fall asleep a minute."

No, you didn't, June thought. *Neither of us did.*
A chill crept through every inch of her.

June had never believed what others told her about the supernatural world, dismissing all religions as just more mind-controlling lies, but she believed there was more to the universe than what was known. Could this river truly be haunted? Had the spirits of Edmund's victims never left this terrible place, or had they followed him home? June knew very well how demons pursued no matter where you fled to. She'd traveled all over trying to escape them, but never shook them off for long, not even with the aid of hard drugs, alcohol, and aggressive sex. Her grandparents had never left her mind, and not just because she was still wanted for questioning in relation to the crime. Was it possible there was more to this than her conscience trying to lay guilt upon her? Could her grandparents have taken on a new form here in Killen, where they'd been laid to rest after their only grandchild slaughtered them in cold blood?

On that dark day, June had stolen their car and escaped across state lines with the cashbox. When she finally got it open, her heart sank. There'd been only seventy dollars inside. June would never know why it'd been so light. Perhaps Grandpa made a bank deposit before it closed for the weekend, or perhaps it had something to do with June being left home alone. Maybe Grandpa had the bulk of the cash on him, just in case. June hadn't bothered to take his wallet or go through her grandmother's purse. She'd been in too much of a hurry to get out of there, and by the time she'd opened the cashbox, it was too late to go back.

June could *never* go home again. She knew that. But she had ended up back in Killen, searching for a different treasure, one she thought might set her life straight again, or at least as straight as the disaster of her could ever be.

"It's okay, Gary," she said, peering at the storm clouds. "We all have our secrets."

TWENTY-SEVEN

GARY DIDN'T KNOW WHAT TO BELIEVE.
Since his wife's death, he longer recognized or understood the known world, but what of this waking nightmare world he'd just seen upon the river? Its sudden, abrasive arrival had left him shaking. It'd all been so real, as if he'd been inside the school as the mass shooter ended the lives of his family, one of many destroyed on that tragic morning. He wondered if he'd been drugged. He had ingested nothing since coming to the woods. Could there be something in the air, some dust from a wild, hallucinogenic mushroom or toxic mold upon the boat?

Gary doubted there was any substance that could trick the mind as thoroughly as whatever he'd experienced. He hoped like hell there wasn't. But that left only one other explanation.

It wasn't a figment. It was real.

Of course, he couldn't accept that. Lacy's ghost wasn't haunting these hills. Her memory haunted Gary, but that was different from actually *seeing* her. But the gorge had become a blood-caked hall of lockers in vivid detail. It gave him an eerie feeling of premonition, despite the event having already taken place. He felt he was being cautioned against something with a powerful warning meant to rattle him to his core.

And it had succeeded.

Gary didn't want to be on this river anymore. Even his urge to look out for June was dwindling in the face of these cosmic horrors. She was grown enough to make her own decisions, even ones this blatantly terrible. Gary wasn't obligated to chaperon these two on their demented quest to find Edmund Cox... or whatever it was they were looking for. But how could he turn back now? He was too deep into the forest to walk back to town, and truthfully, he didn't want to be alone in these woods. Convincing the others to turn the boat around would be impossible.

He was stuck. He was trapped.

A puff of smoke made Gary flinch before he realized it was just Keith's cigarette. He flinched again when the thunder rolled across the low valley, listening for any hint of a slide guitar. Realizing he was expecting The River Man, Gary had to face that he was losing his grip on reality. Was he really afraid of an old country legend, a backwoods boogeyman meant for campfire stories? Perhaps that was the true purpose of The River Man myth—to drive unwanted newcomers out of Killen. Maybe the locals perpetuated the tall tale to keep their land and bloodlines "pure." Was that why the old bluesman at the juke joint had warned him about it? Was Lightnin' Booba Barlow part of some conspiracy to chase away out-of-towners?

Even if this were true, it didn't explain the visions. Nothing could. The only logical explanations were illogical, leaving Gary at an impasse.

I can't explain what I saw, he admitted to himself. *I only know I don't want to see any more of it.*

"Heads up," June said, pointing ahead. "We're about to hit some choppy waters."

The next bend in the river was even less inviting—another bad omen, mother nature giving them one last hint to leave this place.

Keith spoke with the cigarette still in his mouth. "I figure we can manage if we stick close to the banks. This motor's old but it's strong."

He maneuvered the boat closer to the shore but had to redirect it back into the center of the river to avoid a rock cluster.

The waves intensified and Gary held on with both hands. June crouched at the bow, her knuckles running white as the river berated the small vessel. Gary gritted his teeth. Water splashed into the boat and the bow rocked skyward, making him feel weightless. He was sure they were going to flip over, but the boat settled on the river again and they struggled through the rapids. The sound of the waves was overpowering, but beneath their roar Gary heard the thunder as it transformed into the strum of a slide guitar. The playing was wild and drunken, a surge of distorted music that rattled Gary's core. He wanted to mention it to the others, to see if they heard it too, but the river was too chaotic. The rapids hurled them toward a steep dip in the river where serrated rocks awaited them like landmines.

"Hold on!" Keith shouted.

Gary shut his eyes against the spray. Another wave threatened to capsize them, but the boat pressed through it, and this time when the water hit them it was freakishly warm. Gary opened his eyes to find himself soaked in pinkish liquid. The others were dripping in it too.

Another warm wave struck. This one was the color of cherries. June shrieked—perhaps she could see it was blood too? Gary grunted against his rising fear. The guitar grew louder, the speed of the plucked strings increasing to a furious, electric crescendo. Lightning broke the sky open, and the deep redness returned, casting the valley in its devilish dahlia. The halls of the school did not reappear, nor did the floating dead children, but the river of blood grew thicker, *chunkier*, with bits of flesh and bone rising to the surface in a horrific gumbo that steamed like an eviscerated body in the snow.

"Jesus!" Keith yelled.

June closed her eyes against the frothing gore. Shaking, Gary tried to blink the blood from his eyes. He didn't want to let go of the boat to wipe his face. They descended the slope, and for a moment Gary felt as if they were airborne, but they made it to where the river leveled out. While the waters calmed, they maintained their gruesome contents. Ahead, the river was shaped like a serpent, winding toward a towering cliff that stood blackly against the crimson hellscape. Streaks of lightning raked across the sky even though the clouds had passed. Gary tried to wipe his face now, but every bit of him was just as wet.

"The water…" he muttered.

"Ya'll see it too?" Keith asked.

Gary nodded, as did June.

"Jesus Christ," Keith said. "What is this? Some kind of corral or—"

"Corral my ass," Gary said. "This is *blood*."

"Maybe a bunch of fish got caught in something."

"It's not fish. Keith… I've seen things that look human in—"

"It can't be."

Gary pointed to a swirling kite of skin adrift on the current. "*Look at it!* We're floating through *blood and body parts* for God's sake!"

Keith grimaced. "This must be Edmund's doing."

"*What?*"

"He must've found more victims and tainted the water with their remains. He must be real close now."

"Are you fuckin' *kidding me*? He'd have to kill hundreds of people to turn the river into *this*."

Keith didn't have a response to that. Gary looked to June. She was sitting up in the bow again, staring at the river ahead. Her eyes turned toward the sky—toward the top of the cliff.

Gary called her name, unsure what he even wanted to say to the girl.

"Yeah?" she said without looking back at him.

Gary struggled to find words. "This… this is some spooky shit we've got going on here."

"Yeah," June replied, still staring up.

Gary followed her gaze. Plumes of black smoke rose out of a square mass at the edge of the cliff.

"There," Keith said, pointing. "You see that?"

Gary squinted, trying to get a better look at the shape.

"It's a shack," Keith said. "And there's smoke coming out of the chimney." He patted Gary on the shoulder. "We found it, guys. We found Edmund's home."

***

Keith had seen more than he let on.

As the river had run red and the gore floated to the surface, he'd spotted figures moving on the shoreline, familiar faces poking out of the black woodland like Halloween masks. They were faces he'd never expected to see again, faces he *didn't want to see* again. He supposed most cops were haunted by those they couldn't save, as well as those they'd had no choice but to use force against. These people often returned to Keith's thoughts and even permeated his dreams, but he'd never had *visions* of them.

Once the river evened out, the gray faces slunk back into the shadows. He'd only seen them through the spray of the river while he was still trying to keep the boat from capsizing, so he'd not gotten a good look, but was sure he'd recognized them. It'd been enough to make him cry out. He told himself he was only seeing things, that it may have just been knots in tree bark. But while the faces in the woods had disappeared, the river of blood remained. He wanted to believe it was somehow Edmund's doing, but Gary was right to call that a stretch. Something strange was happening here. Killen was living up to its own legends, and it made Keith uneasy. He was raised Catholic, and while he didn't go to church anymore and was generally agnostic, he maintained a residual fear of God from his childhood. It'd been a long time since he'd prayed, but he whispered one to himself now.

Spotting the shack on the cliff rejuvenated him. The return of his determination to catch Edmund Cox replaced all fear and confusion. Keith was positive the killer was up there, that this was the shack no one else in law enforcement had been able to find. This was going to be Keith's biggest bust ever. He couldn't let some bloody water deter his pursuit. That he felt somehow influenced by this strange world around him didn't mean that was so. And as for the faces in the woods, he wouldn't allow some trick of the eyes to keep him from apprehending an infamous murderer and uncovering his lair, which could contain enough evidence to close several missing persons cases. *Let the blood flow*, Keith thought as he peered into the water. *I will not be denied.*

***

June could have vomited.

The blood was bad enough, but bits of tissue had gotten caught in her hair and she had to pluck them out one by one. She tried to keep the wads of flesh to her fingernails, but some of them touched her fingertips when she flicked them into the water.

Gary was right. This gore really did look human. The river was peppered with skin-toned chunks, hair, offal, and bone fragments. Could Edmund have really tainted this large of an amount of water with fresh victims the way Keith suggested? Maybe it was possible, but it didn't seem probable. June imagined the serial killer she sought, hacking and slashing his way through his old stomping ground, killing off his former neighbors and anyone else unfortunate enough to cross his path. It was a thought that both chilled and excited her. She'd read so much about Edmund Cox, but picturing his crimes in her head would be a diminishment compared to witnessing his wrath in person. It would be like seeing her favorite band play live. Despite the frightening visions and river of carnage, the incredible pull that had driven her here had transmogrified into a force she couldn't deny even if she wanted to. She was so close to him now. She felt like she could sense his presence, that they were already linked by the hand of destiny.

The shack sent a veil of smoke into the vermillion vista. Black puffs twisted around each other, becoming a single dark mushroom cloud. The cliff reminded June of a scythe, an appropriate design for the home of a reaper. Edmund Cox, and others like him, were the ultimate messengers of death, for they delivered the news by initiating the process.

Death bringers. Dark angels. Reapers.

June had been such a creature for her grandparents. They'd raised her, never knowing they were nurturing their own cause of death. There was a morbid poetry to that. Was Edmund's legacy of murder even more poetic? Was he therefore worthy of his groupies? While watching videos of him online, June had hung on his every word. He was so lyrical despite his limited linguistic abilities. The things he said—and the ways he said them—came out like songs, a profound musician writing ballads with the tip of a bloody knife.

She couldn't wait to talk to him.

June had so much she wanted to ask, so much she needed to learn.

About him. About herself.

TWENTY-EIGHT

THE WHITE BIRCH TREES WERE now the color of flayed salmon, and their black knots made visages like the heads of ventriloquist dummies within the drear. The hollowed eyes wept blood, reminding Edmund of a nameless victim he'd taken long ago. While raping her, he'd beaten her head into pavement so hard that the vessels in her eyes burst. He knew the faces in these trees belonged to the souls he'd taken, both in Killen and elsewhere. Their mouths were wide in silent screams, their wooden features contorted into death masks of pain. It delighted him, thrilled him, *aroused* him.

He followed the trail uphill, going deeper into The River Man's dimension, feeling more at home here than anywhere else he could imagine.

This is where I belong, he told himself.

It had become a mantra since his arrival on the Hollow River. Though he'd been confident since his prison escape, it wasn't until his return to Killen that Edmund Cox was assured of his destiny. Now that he was drawing closer to his journey's end, he felt cradled by a predetermined course, as if he were not hiking up to the cliff but being transported there by an unknowable, cosmic energy. His fingertips tingled. His penis and testicles swelled. Despite the cold, he grew slick with sweat. He felt like a boy about to lose his virginity or a star athlete readying to score the game-winning goal. Here, in this unholy macrocosm, Edmund was a staunch champion, and it was time for him to claim his just reward.

A rustle in the brush drew his attention. A small, pale figure fluttered past, half-hidden among the weeping willows. Then another tagged behind. On the breeze, Edmund smelled something like a woman's body after intercourse. It was the familiar scent of a particular darling.

"Lori," he whispered into the brush.

A woman's moan rose from the bushes.

Edmund patted Lori's eye in his pocket. It was warm as freshly baked bread. He moved toward the sound, each moan raising more hairs on his arms and neck. The air before him seemed to quiver, the redness rippling in an oval-shaped vortex like a massive birth canal. Proceeding toward it, Edmund allowed the redness to engulf him, and it transported him from the thicket to a darkened bedroom. Judging by the décor, he guessed it belonged to a young male. On a twin bed, two teenagers were having sex, the girl on top of the boy. He seemed younger than she was—smaller, weaker. Edmund watched the scene from the shadows as if looking through two-way glass, seeing the teens without them being able to see him.

Though she was younger, Edmund recognized the girl as Lori. Then he realized who the boy was. She'd confessed it all to him, to show Edmund they both had their dark sides, insisting her cruelties made them kindred spirits. She'd seduced and manipulated her little brother, using threats, lies, and blackmail to continue raping him. The trauma had caused the boy to develop an eating disorder that ultimately killed him.

"That's my girl," Edmund said as he watched young Lori ride her little brother.

He was about to masturbate to the show when the sound of The River Man's slide guitar echoed from one dimension to the next, causing the vision of Lori's past to dissipate. Edmund stepped back and found himself in the woods again, the swirling redness having deepened. The sky was now a painting of blisters and scabs. The music continued in a slapping rhythm, the *boom-chicka-boom* of southern blues at full stomp. The wails of dying women accompanied it, creating a macabre symphony that tickled him. All of Edmund's victims serenaded him at once, every scream and sob and plea for their lives returning in a black squall. His heart pounded and tears of joy flooded his eyes. He spontaneously ejaculated and bit the inside of his cheek just to taste blood.

Closing his eyes, Edmund took it all in.

"It's so beautiful," he said.

Lori's eye vibrated in his pocket. Edmund took it out, unwrapped it, and placed it in his mouth, facing it outward so his darling could see all that he saw. He continued up the incline. His darling's eyeball tasted of salt and rot, reminding him of when he'd popped it from her skull and tongued the weeping socket. He moved through wraiths of smoke that grew thicker the higher he ascended. The trees bent, creating an awning of tangled branches. When Edmund looked closely, he saw they were entwined with the severed limbs of dead women. They were all slender and yellowed, their fingernails cracked, the nail polish chipped. Some fingers and toes had been torn free from when he'd chewed them off the bone like a mad dog.

The incline grew steep, but the aches in his knees didn't bother him here. Nothing did. Even the kink in his neck from the old bullet wound was gone. All the pain he'd felt throughout a lifetime full of it no longer existed. Edmund was raptured into The River Man's domain. All was well.

When he reached the top, he stood upon the cliff like a pioneer claiming new land. He took Lori's eye out of his mouth, tilted his head back, and laughed victoriously. Standing before the dilapidated shack, Edmund held the eye so Lori could see it once again.

"It's nice to drop in on old friends," he said.

But friendship wasn't what he was after.

Edmund approached the blackened hovel. It was just as he remembered it, with the skulls of extinct animals nailed to the rotting boards, wind chimes made of twine and tiny bones dangling from the roof. Tree branches had been bound using dusty shoelaces and fishing line, making mad effigies that stood like broken scarecrows among the debris. A burning meat aroma combined with a foul, septic stench. The roof seemed askew, and the chimney was crumbling, but Edmund knew it would never collapse, only stay cracked and slumped for eternity. Against the backdrop of red light, the shack was pitch black, like a log cabin at a coal-mining camp. On the porch, the carcasses of exotic woodland creatures were placed like offerings, as if they'd committed suicide in honor of what godless horror lurked within. Horseflies buzzed. The caws of scavenger birds were heard but they went unseen. The music and screams had stopped. There was only the steady roar of the river below.

Edmund peered over the cliff's edge. The Hollow River remained a brook of blood, surging and bubbling in a crimson estuary to oblivion. On an assemblage of stones at the shore below, a woman's bloated body was prone. Her limbs were twisted and snapped, purple with bruises and the early stages of decay. One arm was in a crutch.

A childlike voice whispered through the trees. "Sissy…"

Edmund smiled. He held out Lori's eye so she could enjoy the view.

"The things we do for love," he said.

Then he proceeded to the shack.

TWENTY-NINE

THE DEAD MAN ONLY HAD ONE FOOT.
June stared at the corpse, puzzled. Keith turned off the motor, slowing the boat so they could get a better look.

"Cox's work?" Gary asked.

"Nah," Keith said. "From the looks of this guy, I'd say he's been out here a while."

"Where's his foot?"

Keith sighed in annoyance. "How the hell should I know?"

"Well, did Cox have a thing for taking feet?"

"Sometimes feet, sometimes other body parts. But they're always taken from female victims, not old men. Who knows what happened to this poor son of a bitch? What I'm interested in is the boat, and how it got here."

The rowboat sat on the bank near the rock cluster, half sunk and ruined beside the corpse. June wondered if it belonged to the dead man but had the feeling Edmund had claimed the vessel for his own voyage. Keith was right, though. If Edmund had killed the guy, he must have done it much earlier in the week. The maggots had already made a home for themselves. Keith was also right to say Edmund was close. June wasn't sure if that was Edmund's shack on the cliff, but she felt his presence either way, or liked to think she did. She wasn't certain of anything.

Never had been. It was one of the reasons she'd come here.

She'd also intended to make this trip on her own. Keith and Gary were unwanted additions to her quest, and now that they were close to Edmund, she wanted them around even less. Keith wanted to apprehend Edmund, and June couldn't have that. It would spoil everything if he were sent right back to prison.

She needed to get to Edmund before the others did. Otherwise, she'd have to take care of these two herself. Maybe she could get one of their guns away, but it seemed like too big of a risk. Confident she could make it up the mountainside faster than the men, she decided sneaking off would be best. She just needed an opportune time. Fortunately, she didn't have to wait long.

After seeing the other boat, Keith was convinced Edmund had docked here. "We're going up."

Gary's shoulders dropped. "Keith…"

"Don't start with me. I said we're going up—*now*."

"Hey," Gary said, "I don't have to take orders from you."

"I'm an officer of the law. Don't you forget it."

"Oh, c'mon, Keith! Don't wave your badge at me. Not here. Not now."

"I'm not letting you stay here," Keith said. "You've been itching to bail out since we got on the river. You're likely to steal the motorboat and ditch us here."

"If you had any sense, we'd have all gone back already."

"I'm pursuing a killer here, Chatmon."

"Bullshit. You're chasing shadows. There's a greater evil to this place than just Edmund Cox. It's all around us, Keith. Open your eyes."

As the men argued, June stepped up the slope. The white willows seemed to open for her like curtains. She walked backwards, watching the men. She wasn't concerned with the boat like they were. There would be another way out. June didn't plan to go back the way she'd come; she planned to go forward, to make progress, perhaps for the first time in her life.

Everything would change when she found Edmund.

Nothing else mattered.

***

A mean heat rippled through Keith.

Gary Chatmon was an idiot. Bringing him along had been a mistake. What did he need this asshole for at this point? Gary's usefulness had petered out some time ago. Now he was just a nag and a liability, if not a threat to the manhunt.

"You're a goddamned pussy, you know that?" Keith said. "We're *this close* to Cox and you wanna bail."

Gary stared at him like he was a madman. "Can't you see what's happening here? Unless we're all hallucinating, we've entered some sort of... well, I don't know what. A phantom world or something. Hell on earth. Doesn't that trouble you?"

Gary had a point, but Keith would never concede to it. The imagery along the river was horrific, but he'd vowed not to let it stop him. He wasn't a coward or quitter, not even in the face of the unknown. He was on Edmund Cox's heels now. Even the ghosts and demons of the beyond couldn't drive him away.

"Keith, please," Gary said. "I'm not a spiritual man but being here has made me rethink everything. This place isn't normal. We have to get out of here before it's too late."

Keith shook his head. "It's already too late, Chatmon."

Thunder rumbled, and something warm and wet dropped upon Keith's cheek. A few red dribbles fell upon Gary's shoulders. The men looked up just as the sky opened.

It rained blood.

It came down in a sheet, thick and hot and stinking of copper. Gary's face contorted with abject horror, the fear behind his eyes reminding Keith of a little girl he'd rather forget.

"My God..." Gary said.

Keith's fright was short-lived. Instead of instilling fear, the blood rain angered him. This strange place was doing everything it could to scare him away.

Well, it's not going to work.

"Oh my God..." Gary mumbled. "This... this can't be happening."

But it was. They had tread upon cursed land. It had been the playground of a brutal serial killer, a human ghoul. That alone had given it ghosts. But now Keith sensed it was something more than that. Perhaps Edmund was not the cause of this nightmare realm, but a result of it. Killen had a long history of unbridled violence and depravity. Perhaps there was truth to some of its legends, or maybe all that spilt blood really had opened a portal to Hell.

None of this made any difference. If Keith had to dive into The Devil's mouth to capture Cox, he would do it. He would wade through guts and climb over stacked bodies, walk across hot coals, and take a hundred lashes from Satan's whip.

The River Man is real, he suddenly thought.

He tried to discard the notion as nonsense, but everything he was seeing refused to let him.

I'm not afraid, he told himself, wanting to believe it.

But Gary was deathly afraid. Even in the redness, Keith could see how pale the man had gone, like he was on a slab in the morgue. He seemed lost, hopeless, *broken*. As terrifying as this place was, Keith guessed Gary had brought his own darkness along with him. Pain seemed to emanate from his core. Had whatever trauma from his past made him more susceptible to the red world's intimidation techniques, or was the man just a natural born coward?

"Here you are shaking in your boots," Keith said, "and this teenage girl hasn't complained once."

He turned to point at June, but she wasn't there. Both men looked about the woods, peering through the blood rain as it weakened to drizzle.

"June?" Keith called out.

His voice echoed through the valley. It was the only reply he received.

"Where is she?" Gary asked, a tremor in his voice.

Keith's inner heat cranked. "Why do you keep me asking me all these goddamn questions? How the fuck am I supposed to know where she—" He stopped short, narrowing his eyes at Gary as a thought came to him. "Is this some kind of trick?"

Gary blinked. "Trick? What trick?"

"You got her on your side, didn't you? You knew I wouldn't turn back, so you convinced her to help you so you both could run away."

"What? When would I have done that? You've been with us this whole time!"

But Keith could see the panic in Gary, the way he fidgeted and couldn't keep eye contact.

"You two are trying to trick me," Keith said, the heat encouraging him. "You want to steal the boat and leave me stranded."

"Keith, no. Listen—"

But Keith was tired of listening to this conniving dipshit. Gary was a wimp and a snake, and now, not only was Keith's patience tapped out, but his trust was too. He didn't know what Gary was up to but knew it would be like a knife in the back if he allowed it to happen.

Seething, Keith reached for his pistol.

***

Shocked, Gary crouched for his ankle holster, hoping to beat Keith to the draw. The cop was faster. Before Gary could clear leather, an intense pain burst within his chest like a bomb. He felt the bullet before he even heard the gunshot, and went stumbling backward, rolling downhill until he crashed into a crag, smacking his head on a boulder. He wasn't sure if it was red rain or his own blood that spilled into his eyes. Every breath was desperate. His vision blurred and he worried he might pass out.

"Damn it!" Keith shouted. "Why the hell did you go for your gun?"

Because you drew yours, Gary thought but couldn't say.

"I was gonna march you up that hill at gunpoint," Keith said, "but I wasn't gonna shoot you, Chatmon! You made me do this."

Gary wondered how many times Keith Drakeson had blamed the victims of his violence for his actions. Something told him it was a high number. Prone in the mud, Gary looked up at the cop as he hovered over him.

Keith sneered. "You dumb son of a bitch. You're screwed now, you know that? I hit you dead in the chest."

Gary tried to speak but could only wheeze. He wasn't getting enough air and wasn't sure what to do about it.

"Sounds like I hit a lung from the way you're breathing," Keith said. He shook his head and squatted beside Gary. "You realize what this means, don't you?"

Gary hoped not. Dread coiled around him as the drizzle became mist.

"I'm not supposed to be on duty," Keith said, "all on account of me shooting some other asshole who tried to pull a fast one on me. I can't afford another case of using deadly force."

Again, Gary attempted to reach for the gun at his ankle, but Keith put a knee down on his arm, then placed the barrel of his pistol against Gary's temple. And for all his misery and all his thoughts of suicide, Gary winced in the face of death.

"I could end it for you right now," Keith said, his tone flat and cold. "But someone might've already heard that first shot and isn't sure if it was a gun or thunder or what. Another shot might alert them." His laugh was sardonic, cruel. "But then again, these hicks are probably used to hunters poppin' off rifles, huh? So maybe I just want you to die slow."

Gary tried to speak. Blood filled his windpipe. He coughed it up so not to suffocate. His breaths grew shorter as the pain spread, and his vision blurred, distorting Keith into something malevolent, demonic. Gary looked away, hoping to see his late wife's face among the trees one last time.

There was only darkness.

Nothing but darkness.

***

Keith couldn't believe this.

It was bad enough he'd killed a civilian, but now he had another obstacle in the way of him getting to Edmund Cox. He couldn't leave Gary out here exposed. Despite the Hell this patch of the woods had become, Keith didn't believe it would always appear this way to everyone. The redness would fade and the blood rain would stop, because they weren't permanent fixtures. The hellish world appeared and disappeared, just as it had upon their arrival to this forest. Some hiker or hunter could stumble upon Gary's body and call the police. Keith could toss the body in the river but, looking back at the old man's corpse wedged in the rocks, he didn't like the odds of Gary resurfacing. Someone might have seen them together at the motel or driving through town. They'd both been snooping around Killen at the same time. People were bound to link them. Some might believe Gary was another victim of Edmund Cox, but the modus operandi didn't match the killer's style. For that, Keith would have to chop the body up, and he had neither the time nor the stomach for it.

Dragging Gary off trail, Keith removed one of the man's shoes and used it as a trowel, digging into the earth. The first layer was wet and heavy, but the rest came up with ease, Keith using the shoe as a scoop to stack the dirt aside. He worked furiously, cursing Gary for putting him in this position and slowing him down. Even digging a grave this shallow was time consuming, particularly when the only shovel was men's footwear. Keith also cursed June—wherever the little bitch was. He'd almost gone after her first but was hoping she hadn't seen what happened even if she'd heard the shots. He figured he could cover the body before she could discover what happened. Keith doubted anyone would believe some homeless, teenage, serial killer groupie over a respected lawman, but he wasn't about to risk it. She'd have to be dealt with too.

As he worked, time seemed to bend. What should have taken minutes seemed to take seconds, as if fate had stepped in, a supernatural intervention enabling him to do the impossible. He came to believe that this place wanted him to be victorious, that it wanted to see Gary buried. When he'd finally dug a big enough hole, Keith grabbed Gary's ankles and pulled him into the shallow grave. He barely fit, but Keith wasn't spending any more time on this. June could be getting away, and worse yet, Cox could be getting away. The shot might have alerted the killer and scared him off. Keith liked to imagine Edmund Cox fearing him, and he aimed to make it a reality, but he didn't want his man to escape. He had to hurry.

Keith started tossing dirt over Gary Chatmon, beginning at the feet, and working his way up. The soil collected in the wound on Gary's chest before covering it completely. Keith was sweating but he would be finished soon.

As the first handful of dirt hit Gary's face, he suddenly moaned.

Keith straightened, every muscle tense.

Gary moaned again, turning his head to spit dirt, his eyes still closed.

He's alive, Keith thought. *But not for long.*

He threw more dirt over Gary. The man struggled but his injury had robbed him of all strength. As he gasped for air, dirt spilled down his throat. Keith flung more on top of him. Gary's eyes snapped open, flooded with dread and pain, the eyes of a scared little girl in a dingy apartment, staring back at Keith. He wanted to rip those eyes right out of the sockets. Instead, he upended the shoe of dirt again, covering the eyes and muting the final cry of the dying.

THIRTY

EDMUND DREW THE KEY FROM HIS POCKET.
Shawna's festering lip had fused with Niko's teeth, as had
Daisy's nipple to Lori's finger, stapled by the fingernails of Jessica Hong. The dead tissue was moist, as if the kills were still
fresh.

Reaching for the keyhole at the center of the door, Edmund
tingled, watching the wooden boards throb like inflating lungs.
The cracks oozed blackly. He pushed the key of flesh into the
awaiting hole, just as he'd pushed himself into the holes of his
darlings. The door quaked. A sigh of arctic air escaped the lair,
smelling of brine and animal nests. Edmund put his palm flat
against the boards, the shack twitching as if forged of live insects. He gave it a nudge. The door swung inward, creaking like
cemetery gates, and as Edmund crossed the threshold he licked
his lips, tasting decay in the air.

The inside of the shack was festooned in gray slabs of meat
that hung from the rafters like wet curtains. Horseflies made a
brutal cacophony. The only light came from a wood-burning
stove, illuminating the rawhides that blanketed the walls. In the
corner was an old rocking chair. Though it was empty, it rocked
back and forth, the wood groaning like a ship lost at sea.

Edmund's eyes widened in awe.

All these years later and nothing had changed.

He extended his arms as if ascending into the heavens, and then the bitter cold came for him— the cold and the dark— permeating his soul until it was the only thing left to feel.

***

He awoke in a pond.

The water was warm and frothing, black as hot tar. Above Edmund, an obsidian universe had opened in astral decadence, countless crimson stars glimmering in the vastness like distant suns in supernova. A low, electric hum vibrated his heart—the sound of a strumming guitar.

He began to get up, but soft hands emerged from the pool, caressing his now naked body with bloody fingers, his dead darlings yearning for one last embrace. Edmund batted them away and rose from the murk, his footsteps leaving flaming prints behind him. He had desires of his own.

"I'm here," he told the darkness.

The music became a distorted drone—dirty blues slowed to a dying pulse. In the dim, red light, strange creatures yawned, their roars muted by the guitar's scales. The light changed to a purple hue, like stained moonlight, announcing Killen's phantasm.

The River Man's face emerged from the shadows—his features skeletal, his coal-colored flesh cracked and ashy. His scraggily beard hung across his chest, decorated with bone fragments and twitching wasps, and his wiry, gray hair sat upon his skull like a tumbleweed full of worms. Cataract eyes peered out of a cadaver skull. He wore the same moth-eaten suit with cobwebs stuck to the lapels. His guitar was strapped over his shoulder, and he clutched it with both deformed hands—six fingers at the neck, the other six strumming. Edmund noted there were many more fingernails sprouting from the backs of The River Man's hands—signs of other offerings, other deaths in his name. The popularity of his deals was timeless. The River Man hummed, a sound like owls tainted by crickets, and as he sang, his voice crackled with static. His song had no words, only guttural howls, and as he crooned on, spittle fell from his lips and boiled on the floor like acid.

The music surged through Edmund like he was sitting in the electric chair. His limbs trembled and his mouth opened in a blend of bliss and bright pain. His flesh became like the rind of an orange. What others would call horror, he'd learned to call home.

Hell was Heaven. Death was birth. Murder was love.

As the song ended, piercing guitar feedback circled his head until a hollow silence was all that remained.

Edmund approached the towering man-creature. He'd never been certain who or what The River Man was, if he should be considered a poltergeist or devil or something else entirely, a beast that could not be named or categorized. He supposed no one knew—perhaps not even The River Man.

Edmund announced himself. "Killen's favorite son has returned."

The River Man tilted his head. His breaths made clouds of red mist, as if his lungs were filled with blood.

"Been a long time," Edmund said, smiling in the face of evil. "But I'm back."

The River Man remained stoic. Edmund rolled his shoulders, determined. He'd come too far and done too much to be denied.

"I come for what I done earned," he said.

The River Man's voice was deep and raspy. "And what is it you believe you've earned, Edmund?"

Every syllable rattled Edmund's ribcage. Though The River Man wasn't loud, his voice had aftershocks like a bomb. Edmund shook off the feeling of being punched in his solar plexus but couldn't shake what The River Man had said. That he might be unaware of Edmund's accomplishments seemed impossible.

"I've taken dozens and dozens of lives," Edmund said. "Taken 'em hard too. Collected many a darlin'."

The River Man only nodded.

"And I done sent ya my best one," Edmund went on. "Sent my Lori. She was special. She was *willing*."

Again, The River Man nodded, a sound like a beehive escaping his throat.

"Her wish granted mine," Edmund said. "I escaped that cage they done throwed me in. Now I've come on home. Come to see you."

The River Man stroked his beard. Insects writhed within the briar of it. "And what is it you've come back for? Tell me what it is you think you deserve."

"Power."

"Power." The River Man flashed a rictus grin. "Your power comes from within. Its source is the beast of your very soul, which is forever in frenzy. Yet you consider yourself worthy of more?"

Edmund stepped forward. "I know I am. Of all the blood spilt durin' Killen's history, not one has made that river run red more than me. I delivered pain and death in spades. I'd say I was the best investment you ever made, sure 'nuff."

The River Man's teeth chattered like dice, and Edmund wasn't sure if he was grinning or snarling. The mutant hands opened as if cradling an invisible box, moving closer to Edmund. He had to resist the urge to flee. The River Man's hands fell upon either side of Edmund's face. They were cold as icicles and had the feel of tree branches. The River Man stroked Edmund's cheek with the back of his hand, the legion of yellowed fingernails and toenails grazing his flesh, so sharp they shaved away a bit of stubble.

"You are a true son of Killen soil," The River Man said. "Of that there is no question. But there is more for you to know, and more work to be done."

Edmund's eyebrows drew closer together. "More work? You mean more killin'?"

The River Man drew back his hands and the odor of spoiled milk wafted up at Edmund.

"All the people I murdered," Edmund said, "all I done gave you. It still ain't enough? How's that?"

"Because you didn't come back alone."

Edmund glowered.

"There are other souls on this river," The River Man said, "souls who have their hearts set on you. Their fates are interlinked with yours. Therefore, your work remains unfinished."

"What souls? Who's come after me?" He snorted a laugh. "Cops? Feds? Maybe they done brought out the National Guard this time, huh?"

"There's more to it than that. Much more."

Edmund stood up straight, fists clenched. "Just tell me who to kill. I'll gut 'em like a catfish or get sent to Hell tryin'."

The River Man was unamused. "You must make your own decisions in that regard. Those who come to me make their own choices. They must be *willing*."

Of course, Edmund knew that. He'd known it since he was a little boy, hearing tales of those who'd gone to make a deal with The River Man. Edmund thought he'd made his intentions clear from the start. He aimed to kill and kill again. He was an agent of suffering, of unlimited terror and death. His only goal was to torture the innocent and leave their loved ones in everlasting grief. If there were other victims to take, he would do so not just willingly, but gladly. Whoever had followed him upriver would pay with their bodies first, and then their souls. The River Man insisted these pursuers were connected to Edmund's destiny, but Edmund aimed to make them part of his legacy.

"How many?" Edmund asked.

"No more than you can handle."

The purple light faded.

"All I gotta do is kill 'em?" Edmund asked. "Then the power will be mine?"

As The River Man slunk back into the darkness, he offered Edmund Cox one last comment. "Your power is your own, Edmund, just as my power is my own. Never confuse the two."

The blackness engulfed the bluesman, and Edmund did not breathe or blink as the shadow dissipated. A chill coursed through him after The River Man's last words. Though Edmund hadn't mentioned the extent of the power he sought, The River Man already knew. It was as if Edmund wasn't the first to play this game, and now he guessed he wasn't. But surely, he was the one most worthy.

Edmund Cox thought he should be the new demon of the Hollow River.

He deserved to become The River Man for a new generation of killers.

THIRTY-ONE

JUNE FOLLOWED THE SMOKE. It flowed like lava down the hillside, a trail unto itself. The sulfurous odor did not deter her, nor did the ominous nature of everything around her. She'd sooner meet her doom than let Edmund get away. He was here—she was certain of it. At last, she'd tracked down the only man that mattered anymore.

The caw of unseen birds reminded her of the blue jay she'd found on her grandparent's lawn when she was eleven. It had stunned itself by flying into the sliding glass door. June had picked it up carefully, and when she felt it breathing, she'd carried it to the shed and put the bird on her grandfather's work bench, placing its head in the vice grip, and crushed it until its brains oozed out its eye sockets. The bird's wings had fluttered beautifully as it perished by her hand.

Similar memories filled June's heart as she ascended the mountain, coming to mind without conscious effort. She recalled the boy who'd been sweet on her in the ninth grade, and how she'd promised to go on a date with him if he proved his love by swallowing a fistful of thumbtacks. He'd obliged, but instead of getting a date with June, he'd ended up in the hospital. She thought of the suckers she'd stole from since running away from home, and all the decent people who'd tried to help her that she ultimately betrayed, ripped-off, and hurt. Most of all, she thought of her grandparents, and the look of shock and heartbreak on their faces as they'd died. These memories brought her no joy—nothing did—but she also had no remorse for the evil things she'd done. What was the point of being hard on herself? It'd gotten so she didn't even think of these actions negatively anymore.

A gunshot sounded, freezing her. June turned her head back the way she'd come. She thought she heard Keith speaking but couldn't be sure. That meant she was a respectful distance away from the men now. She wondered what had happened but didn't dwell on it. Keith and Gary didn't concern her. If anything, she hoped they were killing each other. It would be one less thing for her and Edmund to concern themselves with.

Continuing her uphill trek, June peered through the redness at a black shape behind the treeline. Her breath caught as she realized she'd spotted the shack. She tingled inside and moved faster, trudging through the brush, and as she reached the plateau, she saw the silhouette of a man against the blistered sky. He was leaving the shack and heading toward the woods opposite her. Wondering if it was Edmund, June wanted to call out to him, but she had to be cautious. It might be Keith or Gary or some backwoods hick. She watched the tall shadow enter the thicket, then scurried her way to the cliff like a feral creature.

June paused before the shack, taking in the grim sight. The morbid decorations made her eyes go wide with curiosity, with enchantment. She felt no fear, only desire, a yearning she could not give a name to. The strange lure she'd felt all along the riverside was now at its peak. June's extremities tingled, her stomach filling with firecrackers. Her whole life had been a painful march toward this moment—to this shack on the edge of the world.

The front door had been left open a crack.

As June stepped upon the porch, the boards seemed to yield to her footfalls, as if she were walking through moist clay, but when she looked down, there was only rotten wood beneath her. She couldn't identify the species of the skull that hung upon the door like a giant knocker, but the images tattooed upon it were clearly a map of the river and, more specifically, of the route she'd taken to get here. The shack's planks swelled and retreated like a breathing chest, reeking of blood and sex and gun metal and human waste.

June couldn't help but tremble. She placed a single finger on the door, but it was enough to push it open. It gave her the weird feeling she'd been expected.

Though the interior resembled a small smokehouse, with fresh meat and tanned skin hanging from the rafters, June's eyes went to the skeletal figure in the rocking chair. He held an acoustic guitar with deformed hands, fingering a haunting melody as June stepped inside. Though he was half hidden in shadow, she could see he was monstrous, a freakish old man the color of ink. The wood-burning stove crackled and popped beside him, the reddish flames making the walls seem to dance and distort. It wasn't until the door closed behind her that June realized she'd come all the way inside.

She knew the song he was playing. As a child, her grandmother had sung it to her before bed. Though this strange man didn't sing the lyrics, June remembered them, and mouthed the words.

Hush-a-bye, don't you cry. Go to sleep ye little baby. Yes, go to sleep, my little baby.

She stepped closer to the nebulous figure.

Way down yonder, in the meadow. There's a poor little lamby. Bees and butterflies, flitter 'round her eyes. She's cryin' out for her mammy.

The hypnotic tune snared her into its web—*his* web—and June sang aloud.

"*Hush-a-bye, don't you cry. Go to sleep ye little baby. Yes, go to sleep, my little baby.*" Though she didn't intend to, the lyrics changed as she sang them. "*Way down yonder, by the river. Lies a poor little lamby. Maggots, worms, and flies, burrowed in her eyes. She's cryin' out for her...*"

As she sang, her voice deepened, aging until she sounded as her grandmother had. Hearing Gramma's voice coming out of her own mouth caused June to gasp, and she stopped singing just as the shadowy man played the song's final chords. The sound left June empty. She felt as if she had to cry but had long ago forgotten how to do so.

The shadowy man rocked in his chair, the creaking like possum screams. June waited for him to say something, but he only watched her with milky eyes that seemed to glow within the murk of his haggard face.

When June spoke, her voice was her own again, but her words fell from her mouth like ash. "I... I, um..."

The man spoke. "Welcome home."

June quivered. "Home?"

"Killen is your home. Killen and this river. Which have you found more to your liking—leaving or your inexorable return?"

Before this moment, June would have said leaving Killen was her greatest accomplishment. But now that she was so close to Edmund, her decision to come back, despite her having vowed never to do so, took the top spot. She stood within a phantasmic netherworld, talking to a deformed minstrel, the dread coursing through her making her feel more alive than she'd had since her initial escape from this miserable river town.

"I had to come back," she said. "I'm lookin' for somebody."

"And he's looking for you."

June blinked. "He... he is?"

The man nodded.

"You've seen him?" she asked.

Another nod.

"Where?" she asked. "When? Was it him who just left?"

"It was he who let you in."

June looked about the one-room shack. No sign of Edmund or anyone else. She was alone with the ominous stranger.

"The man I'm lookin' for," she said. "He's—"

"Your desire is palpable enough for me to gather you will find him at any cost."

"Yes. Absolutely."

"Then what is your offer?"

June furrowed her brow. "What do you mean?"

"The need for home burns in us all. It is not so much a place as it is an emotion. You seek it, and that desire has led you here, to *my* home. You've come asking for my help, but what do you offer to The River Man?"

June paled. The thought had entered her mind, but she hadn't wanted to believe it. Like any child who'd grown up in Killen, she'd heard all the campfire legends and ghost stories. No matter how much she'd tried to rid herself of anything that reminded her of her hometown, some fears were so ingrained they were irreversible. The River Man was such a terror, driven too deep into the hearts of Killen's children to be expunged.

There are some nightmares so hard-wired into our souls they become a part of us forever, June thought.

All along her journey, she'd felt a sense of dread lying dormant beneath her excitement. As the redness bloomed and the river turned to blood, horror had awoken like a long-slumbering demon aroused by the call of a new master. June could not attribute it to any particular entity, for her previous commitment to atheistic logic overruled any belief in the supernatural. But now that she was in the beast's heart, she could no longer deny she'd passed through a membrane into the Killen behind Killen, a parrel dimension of pain that exposed the ugly river town for what it was. And sitting on the throne of this hellish realm was the poltergeist before her.

The River Man. The Boogeyman. The Demon.

"What do you want from me?" June managed to ask.

"All I require is what's already in you," The River Man said. "You only must let it out. Be who you were born to be. You will know the right token when you find it, for you'll have forged it yourself."

June squinted, trying to understand these riddles. Behind her, the door opened slowly, the redness falling into the shack in a wave of light. The River Man rose from his chair, towering over June—a cold, dark, indifferent god. As the glow revealed the twisted nightmare of his face, he gave her these parting words.

"You cannot expect that which you do not yet understand. There is more to know. Your journey on this river is far from over, and your song remains unfinished."

The redness coiled around June's limbs in undulating beams,

like smoke rolling through mountains, like a river of blood leading to parts unknown. It drew her backward, through the doorway, and as she was propelled, her mind flashed upon the blue jay's bursting head, her young suitor vomiting blood after eating thumbtacks, and the way her grandparent's skulls had burst when she'd killed them.

The door closed behind her.

But now she knew how to open it herself.

THIRTY-TWO

KEITH WOULD FIND THEM BOTH.

He was sure of it.

As he tromped uphill, pistol in hand, his heart thudded and his lungs swelled, the anticipation causing a physical reaction. He smiled as he wiped his brow of sweat, fantasizing about all the things he was going to do.

He would catch Edmund Cox, slap cuffs on him, and pistol whip the son of a bitch until he was raw and bloody. Cox deserved to be punished—not so much for the new victims he'd slaughtered, but for daring to escape prison in the first place. It was a slap to Keith's face, and he never turned the other cheek. How dare Cox break free of Keith's punishment? How dare he be a celebrity with horny, young groupies while Keith was a nobody who had to pay for sex? Keith was determined to drag Cox back into a cage as one whipped little puppy, to break the man just as surely as he'd break the case.

He was also going to break June.

Not just because she was a witness, but because she was a no-good whore for murderers. An ignorant, goth slut who spread her pussy for the cocks of killers. She was young and firm but wanted to waste that tender little body on a disgusting monster. In Keith's eyes, that made her worse than Edmund Cox himself. At least Cox had the excuse of being insane. There was no excusing a morbid tramp who wanted to fuck her way to fame using the vilest celebrity possible. June didn't deserve her body any more than Cox did.

But Keith deserved it—yes, indeed.

June wouldn't be the first teenage girl he'd forced himself upon, but he was going to hurt her more than he'd hurt the others, and that was saying something. During his sexual assaults, he'd broken many spirits, but never any bones. All that was going to change when he got his hands on this little cunt. Once he'd had his way with her, she'd be begging him to take her life just to end her suffering. And he'd gladly grant her wish, but would make sure she went slowly, terribly.

Give up the ghost, he thought.

A rustle in the thicket startled Keith, and he pointed his pistol at a swaying bush.

"June?" he said, a little too aggressively. He calmed his tone, trying to lure her out. "June, it's me, Keith. C'mon out. Everything's okay."

From within the dead shrubs came a soft whimper. Someone was crying behind the bushes. They sounded female, and *young*.

Keith wet his lips. "It's alright. Everything's gonna be just fine, sweetie."

How many times had he used that line on underage girls, stroking their chins to turn their little faces up to his? He needed eye contact if he was ever going to climax.

"You're safe now," he said. "You're safe with me."

A small voice whimpered back at him. "You're mean."

Keith froze, his mouth going dry. He had to put both hands on the gun to keep it from shaking. He peered into the bushes, wondering how it was possible. The voice didn't belong to June. It belonged to an even younger girl, one he knew—one he'd *known*.

"You're *mean*, Mr. Keith," she said again. "*I hate you.*"

The familiar words struck Keith like a dull blade. How could *she* be here? It wasn't possible. As she said it again, he lunged into the bushes, unconcerned by the thorns that tore his clothes and cut into his skin. There was no one there, but he heard the voice again, fluttering through the surrounding wilderness like an owl's call.

"I hate you! *I hate you!*"

Keith seethed. "Shut up!"

He ran deeper into the woods, searching with his pistol held high.

"Shut up, you little bitch!" he screamed.

***

Josh Negus was going to fuck him over.

Keith just knew the bastard was planning to cut a deal, that he was turning himself in before the whole network crumbled, an attempt to gain leniency from the DA. Negus' arrest was inevitable and he knew it, but he also knew if he sold out everyone else, he might just shave some years off his sentence.

Confronting him was mandatory. It would be risky in more ways than one, but allowing Negus to turn rat would be far worse than any repercussions a confrontation might cause. Keith had often cut deals with the man, giving him thumb drives full of pornographic photos only law enforcement had access to in exchange for Negus' goods and services, but he'd also thrown his weight around, using his badge to get what he wanted from the man without having to pay full price.

Keith also got first shot at the newcomers.

That's how he'd first met Olive.

Having purchased the little girl from traffickers for a hefty sum, Josh Negus had planned to auction off her virginity to the highest bidder before putting her to regular work, both with clients and in videos.

Keith refused to let that happen to the eight-year-old. If anyone was going to deflower Olive, it would be him.

Until that point, his youngest one had been fourteen, a girl Negus provided in exchange for the child pornography Keith obtained from the evidence room at the station after the bust of an unrelated pederast. The younger the girls, the more delicious they were to Keith. There was something about taking their innocence that intensified his orgasms. Knowing his actions would obliterate any chance the girls had for a normal life, that their souls would be damaged forever by what he did to them, gave Keith a tremendous sense of power, one even greater than the power he felt over others as a police officer, perhaps even greater than the thrill of taking a life. So, using extortion and blackmail, he'd bullied Negus into giving him first crack at the child, the first of many.

But now the network Josh Negus was involved in had been infiltrated by an undercover officer posing online as a twelve-year-old girl. Several busts were made for child pornography and soliciting minors, but thankfully none of the trafficked children had been discovered. Those at the top of the network kept their human treasures securely hidden in basements and remote locations, the children chained to bedposts and deprived of windows. It wasn't until Bobby Small was busted that word got out someone arrested for child pornography was giving names to the feds. Small was a pimp to child slaves—two boys, ages eleven and thirteen, and one girl, age fifteen. He'd made a fortune forcing them into prostitution. Now his empire had collapsed, and the children had been rescued. Small had never met or dealt with Keith, so there was nothing to worry about on that end, but Small dealt with Josh Negus. It was only a matter of time before he gave up Negus' name, and Keith knew Negus would hand over every name he had once the law kicked down his door.

Keith kicked it down before they could.

As he'd barged in, Negus put up his hands, probably expecting federal agents. Instead, only one lawman entered his apartment, one he knew all too well. When Negus saw the gun, he squirmed.

"C'mon, man," he said, tearing up. "What're you doin'? Don't do this."

Keith closed the door with his foot, holding his aim on Negus. The skinny man trembled in his robe. He wore nothing else, and his red body hair was as scraggily as his goatee. Keith had

never liked the guy, but it was rare for Keith to like anyone.
He did like Olive though, even if she didn't like him.

"Where is she?" Keith demanded.

"Just in the other room, man. S'all good. I can get 'er for ya."
He smiled, begging. "Just take 'er, man. She's all yours any time
ya want it. You know you can count on me for that."

"That's just the problem, Joshy. I *can't* count on you. Can't
trust you for shit."

"Keith, c'mon, dude. If you're worried 'bout me, you ain't
gotta be. Ya don't need to point that thing at me, man. I'm your
boy, remember?"

Keith stepped forward, spun Negus by the shoulder, and
pressed the barrel of his 9mm into the man's back.

"Take me to her," he said.

"She's right in here," Negus said, pointing at the only door
in the hallway.

Keeping his pistol on him, Keith had Negus open the door,
which was locked from the outside. Once Keith saw Olive sitting on the bed in her nightgown, he pulled Negus back into the
hall. Olive didn't even look at them. She only stared at the floor.
It was all the little girl ever seemed to do anymore, no matter
what Keith did to her. He wondered if she was like that with
everyone or only him. The last time they were together, she'd
told him to his face that she hated him, that he was a mean man.
All this despite how gentle he'd tried to be with the girl, never
beating her up or verbally abusing her. Ungrateful brat. In the
end, they really were all the same.

Keith shoved the barrel into Negus' nose. "Who have you
talked to?"

"What? Nobody, man."

"I don't believe you."

"I swear to God, man! Swear on my father's fuckin' grave. I
ain't talked shit to nobody. S'all good, dude. We're safe, I swear.
I even deleted the files ya gave me—all of 'em—and scrubbed
out the hard drives before destroyin' 'em. I got nothin' on you,
man. I mean, not that I would ever want to…"

"You weaselly little—"

Keith punched Negus in the stomach. The smaller man folded into him but didn't fight back. Keith would have liked to put his head through a wall but didn't want there to be any bruises that would show.

"Where's your piece?" Keith demanded.

Negus struggled to speak. "Ya… ya want my *gun*?"

"Let's go get it."

They walked to the bedroom, and as Negus reached for the dresser drawer, Keith jabbed him in the kidneys.

"Don't you dare go for it," he warned Negus.

Keith opened the drawer, snatched the revolver, and tucked it into his waistband. He marched Negus back to the hall, stood him nine feet from the front door, and told him to stay put as Keith walked backwards toward it. Negus breathed a sigh of relief, seeming to think Keith was leaving.

That's when Keith shot him.

Negus shuddered and his back burst blood from the exit wound. Keith shot him again, and when Negus fell dead Keith moved quickly. Olive was crying in her room, and when he unlocked the door and went inside, the eight-year-old looked at him with those eyes that would stay with him always.

If only she'd known just how much he wanted to keep her, to take her home with him, to love and cherish her—at least for a little while. There was so much more she had to offer him. It was a shame he had to do this. He didn't want to, but with something as serious as this he couldn't allow any loose ends, no matter how precious.

Holstering his own pistol, Keith grabbed Olive around the waist and brought her to the hallway with Negus, then drew the dead man's revolver.

THIRTY-THREE

HEARING FOOTSTEPS, EDMUND SPUN AROUND
but saw no one. He lifted his nose to the wind, testing the air, but only detected the chimney smoke of The River Man's shack. He could make it out from where he stood, but a dense line of trees obscured the area, raining black leaves like volcanic ash. Still, Edmund knew he was not alone.

There are other souls on this river, The River Man had said, *souls who have their hearts set on you.*

Edmund changed course, backtracking uphill, toward the shack, toward the others. His skin pimpled from the cold yet sweat sizzled in his hair.

Their fates are interlinked with yours, The River Man had told him. *Therefore, your work remains unfinished.*

The air was electric, tickling him, the thought of these other wayward souls making his mouth water with a wanton ache for violence. His mind fragmented into lush memories—a breast squeezed with razor wire, a throat filled with rebar, a knife twisting inside a vagina. *So many ways to penetrate a body.* He ascended the crags like a man climbing the golden steps to Heaven, the crimson radiance elongating his shadow into a writhing scarecrow.

Edmund Cox was feverishly alive.

As he reached the crest, he peered about the cliff with black eyes. Though the scuffling had stopped, he sensed someone nearby. He stood still before the shack. It pulsed, waiting. Soon the throne would be his. He could feel it just as surely as he felt the handle of the butcher knife in his hand, tacky with blood and stiff as his sudden erection. His body thrummed at the promise of another victim. Edmund wet his lips. He bit the bottom one just slightly, chewing away a thin layer of chapped flesh to taste the metallic flavor beneath.

I have become death, he thought. *I am pain. I am—*

His vanity was cut short as something hard pressed against the back of his neck.

"Don't you fuckin' move," a man said into his ear.

Edmund tensed as he recognized the cold kiss of a gun barrel.

"Drop the knife," said the man.

Edmund weighed his options. Finding too few, he obeyed. The butcher knife clanked upon the rocks at his feet, reminding Edmund of dishes shattering against walls, a fragmented memory from his childhood.

"Hands on your head," the man with the pistol ordered.

Edmund did as he was told, which was alien to his nature.

"Turn around," the man said. "Slowly."

Edmund baby-stepped to face his captor. The man was young, but his eyes were aged beyond his years. Flared nostrils made him look piggish. *A cop*, Edmund thought. The man seemed gaunt, as if this pursuit had drained his life-force, but Edmund detected no fear in him, only fury. This was his dance, and he was leading.

"Surprised to see me?" the man asked.

Edmund was stoic. "I know you?"

The man's face soured. "You... you don't remember me? You gotta be fuckin' kidding."

But Edmund wasn't. He had little need to recall the faces of men—especially cops, who were all the same bland entity. His mind disposed of such useless memories.

"I don't know you from Adam," Edmund said.

The man scowled, insulted. "I'm Detective Keith Drakeson, asshole. I captured you the first time around, and now I've done it again."

Edmund remained deadpan.

"I fuckin' shot you," Keith said.

The old wound in Edmund's neck throbbed at being mentioned. He ground his teeth but kept his mouth closed so Keith wouldn't see it.

"You're not just a sicko," Keith said. "You're a moron to boot. You led me right to your shack."

Edmund grinned. "Ain't mine."

"Bullshit. You just don't want me to get credit for finding it. All those feds combed these woods up and down, over and over, looking for this place. But I found it." He punched his chest with his free hand. "*Me*! Keith fuckin' Drakeson."

"*Pride goes before a destruction,*" Edmund said, reciting proverbs, "*and a haughty spirit before a fall.*"

He glanced at the edge of the cliff. Keith followed his gaze but wasn't distracted long enough for Edmund to make a grab for the pistol.

"Don't give me that backwoods poetry shit," Keith said. "I found you, and now you're gonna pay for everything you've done."

"Is that a fact?"

"Don't mock me, you sick bastard."

Edmund smiled wider. "If ya gonna shoot me, shoot me. But spare me the big hero horseshit. I've heard it all before, and it ain't impressing me or nobody."

The pistol flew so quickly Edmund didn't realize what was happening until the butt of the gun cracked open his forehead. His vision filled with stars, then blood. He stayed standing, but Keith kicked him in the knee, and Edmund lost his balance. The ground raced up at him, black rocks the size of footballs making for a painful landing. Then the barrel of the pistol pressed into his eye socket, the cop spitting on Edmund as he twisted his arm behind his back with more strength than Edmund would have thought the man capable of. Edmund's wrist was cuffed, the sound reminding him of when he'd cracked thirteen vertebrae in one of his darling's backs, paralyzing her.

"I'm dragging you back to Hell, Eddie," Keith said. "I'm gonna put you in a solitary cage so small and dark you'll cry like a baby for the rest of your worthless life. Ready to go even crazier, you sick fuck?"

Edmund considered this. "What is madness to the damned?"

"Jesus," Keith said, scoffing. "You think you're some hot shit don't ya? Talkin' like Charles Manson. Collecting all those sick cunt groupies. Well, you're never gonna fuck a woman again. The only sex you'll be having is with some big Bubba who's even crazier than you. It's your turn to be a victim, Cox. You're gonna feel what it's like to—"

There was a rustling sound just before Keith grunted. The weight of the cop fell upon Edmund, Keith's blood dribbling upon his neck. A drop fell upon Edmund's lips, and he lapped it up as he turned over, shoving Keith off him, hoping to snatch the gun away.

Standing above them was a teenage girl.

She had black hair and blacker eyes. Edmund was instantly struck by her morose beauty and the coldness of her slack expression. In her fist was one of the large rocks, slick with Keith Drakeson's blood. She gazed upon Edmund with quiet awe. Though he tended to forget many faces, he felt sure he knew hers but had trouble placing it. When their eyes met, the girl's lips parted, as if there was something she needed to say but couldn't, as if she'd forgotten how to breathe.

The pistol had fallen from Keith's hand. As the cop stirred in half-consciousness, Edmund took the 9mm away from him. The girl made no move for the pistol and showed no fear when he picked it up. She only stared at him as if lost in a dream, the same way his Lori once had.

Keith had only attached one handcuff. The other swung by the short links, dangling from Edmund's gun hand like jewelry. He rose to his feet. The girl gazed up at him as he towered over her. Even in the red iridescence, he could see she was pale as snow, but it was not fear that had turned her this color. Her pallor was her natural complexion, as if she'd never seen the sun and had no desire to. He stepped closer to her, and as the breeze blew strands of hair across her tender face, Edmund used one finger to draw her hair back and tuck it behind the girl's little ear.

"Hello, darlin'," he said.

Her lips moved, but if she spoke Edmund could not hear her. On the ground, Keith stirred and put his hand to his busted head. His face was now covered in blood, and he blinked it away from his bleary eyes. As he attempted to get to his feet, Edmund returned to the man, pressed the barrel of the gun against Keith's kneecap, and fired.

Keith let loose a high-pitched scream as his kneecap splintered, blood drenching his slacks as bone fragments burst through the fabric.

"Breathe, Keith," Edmund advised. "Taste the pain. Embrace your suffering. You'll be livin' with a good deal of it from now on."

Keith cried and squirmed in the dirt where he belonged.

"Just another squealin' pig," Edmund said, winking at the girl.

She only stared at him, her eyes damp with wonder. As Keith's wailing dropped to gasps for air, Edmund turned his attention to her but kept one eye on the cop.

"Who are you?" Edmund asked her.

The girl's bottom lip trembled. Edmund waited.

Finally, she spoke. "My name's June."

"June what?"

"Audrey. June Audrey."

The last name sounded familiar. Edmund sucked his teeth. "Why'd you save me, June Audrey?"

June gulped hard enough for Edmund to hear it. She stammered. "I... I um..."

Edmund stepped closer. The girl didn't step back.

"How come you look so familiar?" he asked. "I know you?"

She shook her head. "No. Not me."

Their eyes locked.

"You knew my mom," June said.

THIRTY-FOUR

THE BREEZE PICKED UP, and when June's hair whipped across her face, she almost brushed it away, but decided to wait for Edmund to do it again. She'd loved it when he touched her and hoped he would do it some more, forever.

"Your mom?" he asked, brushing her hair behind her ear, his fingertips lingering on her flesh.

June thought of her mother then, sitting silent in the visitation room of the mental hospital, her hair covering her face in a dark curtain, concealing her horrid disfigurement.

"Her name was Elisa," June said. "Elisa Audrey."

She watched Edmund's face change. His eyebrows raised, a sign of a lost memory rushing back. His grin was like a hyena's.

"My, Jesus, my," Edmund said. "Lil' Elisa Audrey. Ya know, your mama holds a special place in my heart. And will 'til my dyin' day. A man don't never forget his first rape. It's just like a first kiss or first car. It's special when you pop that cherry. That first victim stays a darlin' precious one."

June quivered. Edmund was so casual about the pain and suffering he'd dispensed. It was as if he were talking about the weather rather than the ruination of a human being's life—*her mother's* life.

"Thought she was my first murder too," Edmund continued.

185

"See, I left her to bleed out in the woods. That lil' girl barely even had a face no more after I was done with her." He grinned fondly and shook his head. "Wasn't till I heard it on the news that I done found out she were alive. Scared me shitless, I tell ya. I thought for sure I was gonna end up in the slammer. Get put in the 'lectric chair. But I done lucked out. Your mama had gone into shock and never said a word to nobody 'bout what all happened. Never recovered and never told who done raped and tortured her. And with me not havin' any criminal record yet, nobody done suspected me of nothin'."

Edmund smiled up at the sky of blood. June had a burning urge to go to him, wrap her arms around his neck, and drag him in for that first embrace, the first of many.

"What I wanna know is," Edmund said, "how'd you figure out it were me who done it?"

June somehow managed to speak. "I'm not the only one. There're a lot of unsolved rapes and murders in these parts that people attribute to you."

"What people?"

June shrugged. "I've just read articles that say so."

"Alright. But what I don't understand is why you'd wanna save me from this here piggy when I'm the one who done destroyed your mama. Unless, of course, ya only stopped him 'cause you wanna be the one to take me down. Get your revenge for dear ol' mammy."

The song her grandmother used to sing returned to June.

Bees and butterflies, flitter 'round her eyes. She's crying out for her mammy.

"You wanna get revenge on me, girl?" Edmund asked.

June shook her head. At their feet, Keith groaned, holding his shattered kneecap with both hands, his face alive with shock. Edmund didn't even glance at him. His dead eyes stayed on June's, and to her surprise she didn't look away.

"I don't want revenge," she said. "I just want you in my life."

Edmund furrowed his brow but said nothing, waiting for her to say more.

A tear fell down June's cheek. "What girl doesn't want their daddy?"

She watched Edmund's face drop. Silence fell between them then, broken only by the whimpers of the crippled detective and the low thunder that rolled across that lonesome valley, echoing through the deep, black gorges, and rippling the river of blood below.

All her life, June had suffered this void, a hollowness she carried in her broken heart, eating at her soul like a fury of maggots. She'd never really had a mother and had never even known who her father was. Her grandparents fed her well-meaning lies about him, but once she was old enough, she'd figured out the truth on her own. Her mother had been so young at the time of her attack. It stood to reason she'd been a virgin before the sexual assault, and she'd certainly not had sex with anyone after the attack. And the timeline added up with June's age. She had to be the result of her mother's rape. Therefore, her father was the very man that had taken her mother away from her. Though she'd pieced it together in her pre-teens, she'd never confronted her grandparents about it. She was too ashamed to be born from such destruction. In her mind, if she confessed to knowing the truth, her grandparents would resent her even more than they already did. For all their love and sweetness, they must have harbored deep resentment toward her. She was a constant reminder of what had happened to their only child, a living reflection of the foul beast that had left their daughter a disfigured vegetable, an act that tore their family apart. And because June could never feel accepted as part of the Audrey family, she'd begun to wonder if she would be a better fit with her father's blood relations.

But though she'd known her father was her mother's attacker, she hadn't known who he was. Killen was rife with sexual predators, violent offenders, and general creeps. It was a hick town fraught with incest, molestation, robbery, and bloody feuds. This southern soil bordered on primitive, a valley where the reptilian brain could flourish. It wasn't until Edmund Cox was captured and tried for all those murders that June gained a likely suspect. The way he'd tortured and mutilated his women mirrored what the unknown assailant had done to June's mother, only to even worse extremes. Mom had been this un-hinged artist's early canvas, and he'd gone on to paint works of horror far grander than she.

June had become obsessed with the case then, reading and watching everything she could about the notorious serial killer. She'd long felt an inexplicable darkness within herself, a black energy she could not define or control. Though she'd never be-lieved this to be a malevolent entity or demonic possession, she'd always felt predestined to behave in a manner humans found dreadful, loathsome, *evil*. Discovering her ancestry, it had all begun to make sense at last.

She was the offspring of a monster.

How many letters had she written to Edmund, only to tear them up and never send them? Somehow words failed her. June could never quite capture what she felt deep in her guts. She assumed he must receive countless letters from deranged yahoos claiming to be his children. Some people would do anything to insert themselves into the lives of a celebrity. But June wasn't like that. She didn't want to be close to Edmund because of his fame. She wanted him because she was certain he was the one person in this rotten world who could possibly understand her.

"My daughter?" Edmund asked.

June nodded as another tear rolled down her cheek. Behind Edmund, the sky raged in swirls of burgundy, the blistering scabs of ancient gods.

"You got my eyes, child," her father said.

And then she was lost to him, lost and happy.

THIRTY-FIVE

KEITH WINCED AS THEY LIFTED HIM, slinging his arms across their shoulders like he was a wounded soldier. Edmund was saying something about work that needed to be finished. June seemed to understand though Keith did not. And why shouldn't she? Keith had heard what the girl said. She was Edmund Cox's daughter, or so she claimed. Keith didn't want to believe it, but something told him it was true, and looking at them side by side, there was a resemblance Keith couldn't deny. It was more than just their physical features. The two emitted the same degenerate energy, each a brooding force of nature, twisted by their very blood. These two were born into Killen. They could know only horror and only find pleasure in causing suffering and death.

They dragged Keith up the shack's steps. He wanted to fight against them but was too dizzy and weak. His dented skull scrambled his thoughts and every little movement sent agony through his leg. He hopped on one foot as the maniacs cradled him, trudging toward his doom. He knew once he entered this shack he would never leave. This was Edmund's house of horrors. How many unknown victims had died here? How many bodies were stored within these withering slabs of wood? Keith figured he would soon be just another corpse buried under the floorboards. He could only hope Edmund would make it fast. The killer tortured his female victims but had never seemed to get off on it with men. His sadism was psychosexual, a feral thing. Keith could only ask God for a swift death. He just didn't want to suffer any more than he already had.

No, he thought. *You can't think like that. You can't give up. It's not over yet.*

But it was. Even if by some miracle he got the upper hand on these lunatics, trekking all the way back to his car would be impossible in his current state. He would have to crawl, and even that would be excruciating.

You can't give up! You'll find a way. You can scoot downhill on your butt and make it to the boat. Then you can get help.

But he didn't believe that no matter how deeply he wanted to, and when the door to the cabin came open, Keith realized his horrors were only beginning.

Bones hung from the rafters in macabre sculptures and tanned hides were stitched into pinwheels of the dead. The smell of decay rose out of the dark, a foul waft from a thousand opened tombs. The strange buzzing made his teeth grind. It sounded like they were entering a wasp's nest, but there were no insects. The redness outside the shack was not present here. In this country shack, there was only a moonlike glow that bruised further to purple the deeper they ventured inside. It illuminated nothing. They'd entered a vortex as black as midnight. Its coldness made Keith's teeth chatter, and then there was the sudden sensation of falling, of his innards rising into his throat. Crimson stars appeared in the vastness, spattered across an onyx universe like a spray of blood. The silence was reminiscent of a snowy day, the void eating all sound—even Keith's screams of terror—until an out of tune guitar strummed.

The noise made the air quiver like heat waves over a desert highway. Reverberations shook Keith's ribcage, causing his heart to skip a beat, and his limbs became jelly. His bowels churned. His skin pimpled.

Splashing into an ink-like pool, Keith realized he was alone. He looked around for Edmund and June but saw only shadows in this endless ruin. Slowly, other faces appeared—the tiny little faces of all the little girls he'd enjoyed. They wore the whorish makeup Josh Negus had adorned them in—cherry lips and rouged cheeks, clownish against their tender, chalk-white flesh. Their makeup ran from tears, smeared with the warm saliva of men like Keith.

He shuddered as their naked, bruised bodies were revealed to him. Many of the girls had been starved into obedience—customers didn't like being kicked and bitten. The concubines had to be punished until they learned to play nicely with the older boys who rented them.

"You're mean," the children said in unison, voices buzzing like horseflies. "We *hate* you."

Keith's mouth fell agape. "I didn't... didn't mean to..."

The guitar serenaded the terrible scene with haunted blues. The children began to dance in sluggish, drunken movements, their nubile bodies freakishly contorting. Even with the music blaring, Keith could hear their bones snap and break. Their heads twisted about on their necks, knees and elbows inverting, tongues elongating into pink whips of diseased tissue. And yet they danced on like horrible human crabs. The purple light swelled. A cruel wind blew, coating the little girls in an azure frost. They stopped in place like ballerinas on a jewelry box, their knotted bodies gone snowy white with touches of blued corpse flesh hiding beneath the glaze. With another strum of the guitar, they shattered into chunks of ice, the red crystals of their frozen blood exploding when they hit the ground.

Keith screamed and it all disappeared.

A towering man-creature emerged from the phantasmagoria.

Fear choked Keith, making him fall silent. The six strings of the minstrel's guitar gleamed like knives in sunlight, and he fingered them with deformed hands, his blackened teeth chattering in percussion.

He's real, Keith realized. *My God, he's actually real.*

Keith's teeth chattered too. "Riv... River Man."

Despite his dread, Keith was relieved to see The River Man, because if the legends were true, he could strike some sort of

191

deal. He could get his knee back. He could capture Edmund Cox. He could bash June's head in with a rock to show her how it felt and then bend her over a log and sodomize her. He could get out of this *alive*.

"Holy shit," Keith said as he gazed upon the strange djinn. "You're him."

The River Man said nothing.

"I wanna make a deal," Keith said, not wasting time.

The River Man's lips curled back from rotten jaws. "You've been making our deal all your life, Keith."

That The River Man knew his name made Keith swallow hard.

"I'll do whatever it takes to get what I want," Keith said.

"That's nothing new, now is it?"

"I'm just saying I'm willing to—"

"Precisely, Keith. You're *willing*. It's the only way to come to me."

The darkness seemed to swarm with invisible serpents, making Keith even colder. The River Man was speaking in riddles the way Keith detested, causing him to clench his fists. Even in the face of such a horror, it was rage that took Keith Drakeson, always rage.

"You come to me with wrath," The River Man said, reading him with ease, "just as you brought wrath down upon the souls of the young and fragile. All that sweet innocence broken by your unquenchable thirst for corruption. A sadist's lust can never be satiated."

Keith's brow lowered. "I know what I am."

"And yet you persecute other monsters."

"Now wait just a minute. If you're talking about Edmund Cox, there's a world of difference between what he does and what I do."

The River Man's milky eyes churned. "The cobra looks down upon the rattlesnake, yet both are filled with venom."

Keith gritted his teeth. He'd had enough. "Just *tell me* what I need to do to get what I want."

"And what is it you want, Keith?"

"Everything," he said. "I want *everything*."

"Greed." The River Man flashed his skeletal grin. "The same old song. But what do you offer The River Man?"

Keith couldn't breathe. The question was almost like a threat, because he'd come empty-handed.

"I didn't expect to…" he mumbled. "I mean… I didn't know what to…"

The River Man's smile widened, mocking Keith. "Such promise in you, and yet you offer nothing."

Keith tried to rise from the fluid but was too crippled to do so. He could only sit there with his legs out like a discarded marionette. He shuddered, confused.

"Hold on" he said. "What does that mean and… *damn it*! I thought you were supposed to be some kind of genie. Just *tell me* what I gotta do!"

The River Man only smiled wider, his face contorting ghoulishly, smoke billowing through the gaps in his arrowhead teeth. A shadow moved behind Keith, followed by another. The hairs on his body stood, and he turned his head just slightly, curious, and yet not wanting to see what he now knew. From behind, a heavy hand fell upon his shoulder.

"Don't ya know how to sell yourself to a devil?" Edmund Cox whispered in Keith's ear. "Ya gotta offer up your soul, boy."

The tip of a blade pierced Keith's throat just slightly, a drop of blood rolling down his neck, becoming one with his perspiration. A second figure emerged from the greater dark, Keith's pistol in her hand.

June wore the sort of coy smile that at one time would have excited Keith. Now he knew the girl too well to embrace any erotic illusions. In her hooded eyes, he saw only the shadow of death.

Keith turned to The River Man, the demon being his last hope.

"Please," he begged. "Don't let them do this. I'll do anything you want."

"You already have," The River Man told him. "Over and over again you've done it, in all those dark, little rooms, with all those frail, little bodies." The crimson stars flickered, illuminating the drear and giving Keith glimpses of all those children watching from the outer dark. The River Man gestured to them. "A hundred candlelight vigils for help that never came."

"I can do more," Keith vowed. "Much more. I'll snatch them from schoolyards. Use my position as a police officer to gain their trust. I'll rape 'em real good for you—*repeatedly*. Shove things inside them. Throw 'em in dog crates and make them die slow. I'll do it all for you, I swear it. Shit, I don't care! *Fuck* those little girls! They all grow up to be miserable cunts and cock-teasers, anyway. So what does it matter? I don't *fucking care*!"

Cold silence was The River Man's sole reply.

Edmund snickered at Keith. "So cute. You're as bad as me."

"Worse," said June.

Keith sneered at them. "I'm nothing like you."

"There is an inequality," The River Man said. "Such promise in you, Keith, and yet you've failed to understand the difference between obtaining an offering and being one."

Keith inhaled, a silent scream.

The butcher knife pressed deeper into his throat, and June walked up to him and put the barrel of the pistol against his good knee.

Keith shrieked. "Wait! *Don't!*"

She fired. His remaining kneecap burst, and pain raced up his leg, into his groin, and shook him throughout.

Edmund smiled at his daughter. "Whatta ya say, darlin'?"

She smiled back at her father with a look of love far stronger than anything Keith had ever known.

"Well, Daddy," she said, "I say *Pieces of Police Detective's Body Found in Woods*."

Edmund laughed. "That's my girl." He gazed down at Keith. "Now you see that, boy? You wanna be front page news? Looks like you're getting your wish after all."

Keith screamed. June shot him in the left shoulder, then the right. He tried to put up his hands to defend himself but couldn't move his arms anymore. June stepped on his wrist and fired another round through his palm. Keith writhed in agony. Edmund got down on his knees beside him and pressed the tip of the butcher knife under Keith's right eyelid.

"Don't," Keith whimpered. "Don't kill me…"

Edmund scoffed. "I ain't gonna kill you. She is."

He nodded toward June and the girl's eyes glowed like crimson stars.

THIRTY-SIX

THEIR OFFERING DISMEMBERED, the father and daughter stepped into one another, entwining like vines. June placed her palms against Edmund's chest, the blood making them stick, binding them just like the Cox blood pulsing through their veins. Her father's hands fell upon her shoulders, the fingers that had prodded the wounds of so many screaming women now warming June in all that arctic blackness. She grazed his chest, her fingernails packed with red bits of the dead cop's flesh, and they simply breathed one another, Edmund's foul breath wafting over her porcelain doll face, her lips parting in a little sigh.

June's father pulled her in closer, one hand at the small of her back, the other snaking into her raven hair. He crouched to brush his cheek against hers. Stubble scratched her like sandpaper, and she wrapped her arms around him, gently putting her nails into his back, and when he leaned in, June opened her mouth to accept his tongue. His erection pressed against her belly, wetting her, and in the squalid darkness of The River Man's realm, the Cox family stripped nude and lay within the gore and tar, expressing their love physically amongst the red ruin of their victim.

The River Man serenaded from the shadows.

"Way down yonder, by the river. Lies a poor little lamby. Maggots, worms, and flies, burrowed in her eyes. She's cryin' out for her daddy."

And she did. Again and again. Thrusting and sweating in the moist pit of their love. And when their passions were satiated, they dressed and exited the shack, stepping out into the pale, gray dawn of a new day, smiling at all the fresh treasures the world offered, and the many delectable horrors they would offer it in return.

The Cox family had accepted their reward.

Now they would embrace their new task.

THIRTY-SEVEN

LOVE IS A FUNNY THING. You know that, right, Lori?

I reckon you must, given all ya done did for me, knowin' who I was—what I was. Just know you'll always be my darlin'. That much is true. But blood is thicker than water, even thicker than the water that flows through that ol' river.

Without you, I never woulda found her. I'd of been locked up in that human zoo. Never woulda been reunited with my baby girl. Never woulda tasted her. Never woulda known this kind of love. And knowin' she's only with me cause a you makes me love ya even more, my Lori. You're one hell of a matchmaker. Now and then, I promise I'll think of you when I'm inside her. It's the least I can do.

Here I'd thought my journey had come to an end, but that old man river just keeps rollin' along, darlin'. I thought I was gonna take the throne where that cliff hangs off the blood red sky, but my time has not yet come. The River Man knows best. Always has and always will. My work is not yet done, and my daughter's work has just begun. I must mentor her, raise her right, show her how it's done. 'Cause she's my little bucket and I'm here to fill her with all I know and all my love. I'll hold her little hand till my time comes, be it my seat upon that throne of all horrors or deep down in the sweet peace of the grave.

I hope you're watchin' from your own lil' corner of Hell, Lori, and I hope you're happy. You oughta be. You done real good, darlin'. Better than

I ever woulda dreamed.
    So you just sit back and enjoy the show.
    Our next victim will be dedicated to you.

Acknowledgements

Thanks to all my readers and fans, who mean more to me than I can ever express. Special thanks to everyone who read, reviewed, and shared *Gone to See The River Man* on social media, helping to make it the international horror sensation it has become.

Thanks to Jonathan Butcher, Mona Kabbani, Aron Beauregard, Norman Prentiss, C.V. Hunt, Lynne Hansen, Edward Lee, Bryan Smith, Brian Keene, Daniel J. Volpe, Wile E. Young, Kristopher Rufty, Ryan Harding, Gregg Kirby, Josh Doherty, Tim Lebbon, and Jack Ketchum.

Special thanks to Junior Kimbrough, Jimmy "Duck" Holmes, Muddy Waters, Robert Belfour, R.L. Burnside, Buddy Guy, Robert Johnson, Howlin' Wolf, Rev. Gary Davis, Mississippi John Hurt, Geeshie Wiley, Son House, Johnny Cash, Lead Belly, Skip James, Blind Willie Johnson, B.B. King, Roosevelt Booba Barnes, John Lee Hooker, Katie Webster, Ry Cooder, Willie Dixon, Hank Williams, Fenton Robinson, Tom Waits, Blind Willie McTell, Furry Lewis, Koko Taylor, Freddie King, Bukka White, Bo Diddley, Sam Chatmon, Nick

Cave & Warren Ellis, Mississippi Fred McDowell, Willard Grant Conspiracy, and Nick Drake for their inspiring music.

Extra special thanks to Bear.

And thanks to my best buddy Thomas Mumme—always.

About the Author

Kristopher Triana is the multiple award-winning author of *Gone to See the River Man, Full Brutal, The Thirteenth Koyote, They All Died Screaming,* and many other terrifying books. His work has been published in seven languages and has appeared in many anthologies and magazines, drawing praise from Rue Morgue Magazine, Cemetery Dance, Publisher's Weekly, Scream Magazine, and many more.

He lives in New England.

Signed books and merch: TRIANAHORROR.COM
Newsletter: kristophertriana.substack.com
Instagram: Kristopher_Triana
Facebook: Kristopher Triana
TikTok: Kristophertriana
Twitter: Koyotekris

Printed in Great Britain
by Amazon